Forgotten

Patricia H. Rushford

Books by Patricia Rushford

Young Adult Fiction

JENNIE McGRADY MYSTERIES
1. *Too Many Secrets*
2. *Silent Witness*
3. *Pursued*
4. *Deceived*
5. *Without a Trace*
6. *Dying to Win*
7. *Betrayed*
8. *In Too Deep*
9. *Over the Edge*
10. *From the Ashes*
11. *Desperate Measures*
12. *Abandoned*
13. *Forgotten*

Adult Fiction

Morningsong

HELEN BRADLEY MYSTERIES
1. *Now I Lay Me Down to Sleep*
2. *Red Sky in Mourning*
3. *A Haunting Refrain*
4. *When Shadows Fall*

Forgotten

Patricia H. Rushford

BETHANY HOUSE PUBLISHERS
MINNEAPOLIS, MINNESOTA 55438

Forgotten
Copyright © 2000
Patricia Rushford

Cover illustration by Sergio Giovine
Cover design by Lookout Design Group, Inc.

Library of Congress Catalog Card Number 99–050486

ISBN 0–7642–2121–3 (pbk.)

Published by Bethany House Publishers
A Ministry of Bethany Fellowship International
11400 Hampshire Avenue South
Minneapolis, Minnesota 55438
www.bethanyhouse.com

Printed in the United States of America by
Bethany Press International, Minneapolis, Minnesota 55438

For my grandchildren,
Kyrstin, Hannah, Jonathan,
Christian, and Andrea.

And especially for Chenayla and James,
who may be gone,
but will never be forgotten.

PATRICIA RUSHFORD is an award-winning writer, speaker, and teacher who has published numerous articles and more than thirty books, including *What Kids Need Most in a Mom, The Jack and Jill Syndrome: Healing for Broken Children,* and *Have You Hugged Your Teenager Today?* She is a registered nurse and has a master's degree in counseling from Western Evangelical Seminary. She and her husband, Ron, live in Washington State and have two grown children, nine grandchildren, and lots of nephews and nieces.

Pat has been reading mysteries for as long as she can remember and is delighted to be writing a series of her own. She is a member of Mystery Writers of America, Sisters in Crime, Romance Writers of America, and several other writing organizations. She is also the co-director of Writer's Weekend at the Beach and teaches at writers' conferences and schools across the country.

1

"We're gonna have a blast tomorrow!" Lisa Calhoun, Jennie's cousin and best friend, pulled the bulk of her coppery red curls over her left shoulder and wove a strand between her fingers. "I can hardly wait."

"Me either." Jennie McGrady eased her red Mustang into the right lane of the freeway leading from Oregon City to Lake Oswego. Their "blast" was a hike along the Lewis River in Washington State, not far from Mount Saint Helens, the famous volcano. Jennie's friend Scott Chambers and Lisa's new boyfriend, Gavin Winslow, would be going with them.

"I'll bet you're excited to see Scott. Will he be at the swim meet?"

"No." Jennie sighed in disappointment. "Didn't I tell you? He called last night. Couldn't get time off." Jennie put the visor down to block the late afternoon sun. Not that she minded the sun. It was a welcome relief after a week of chilling November rain.

"Bummer. Gavin was looking forward to having him spend the night. He's still coming, isn't he?"

"Yeah, but he has to work later than he thought tonight. Something about getting a new exhibit ready for the weekend." Scott worked at the Coast Aquarium in Newport. "He's getting up super early and promised to be at my house at eight-thirty Saturday morning."

"Where are you going?" Lisa asked when Jennie made

a right into the shopping mall instead of going straight on the crowded boulevard.

"To the bank. I promised Mom I'd deposit some checks for her on my way to school this morning, but I forgot." Jennie wrinkled her nose. "Don't tell Mom. She will *not* be happy. I've had over a thousand dollars worth of checks in my glove box all afternoon." The checks were from her mother's part-time accounting business.

"Yikes." Lisa cringed. "Don't worry. I won't say anything. But how could you forget something like that?"

Jennie shrugged. "I was going over my study notes for the history test on my way to school. By the time I remembered the deposit I was halfway through the test. The worst part is that I left the checks on the front seat where anyone could see them."

"Jennie!"

"I know." She winced. "Fortunately, they were still there after class. I put them in the glove box and locked it." She'd also checked her doors twice to make sure they were locked.

Jennie pulled into a parking place in front of the bank next to an armored truck. Reaching across Lisa, she opened the glove box and pulled out the deposit envelope. "Are you coming in with me?"

"No." Lisa dug through her purse and came up with a nail file. "I'll wait." She flashed her red-tipped fingernails. "Broke a nail."

As Jennie opened the door, Lisa reached for the knob on the radio and pressed it, filling the car with the music of Michael W. Smith. Jennie was tempted to stay and listen, but she really needed to get that deposit made.

Shoving against the heavy glass door, Jennie stepped inside, passing a uniformed man with a gun drawn.

A gun? Jennie's heart slammed into overdrive. *What's going on?*

The scene inside the bank played out like a slow-motion movie. Two men and two women lay facedown on the floor. Having had first-aid training, Jennie's first instinct was to check them for injuries. At the same time, her brain registered imminent danger.

"Freeze." Jennie felt the barrel of the guard's gun sink into her side.

"But—" She turned to explain she was just a customer. Her words turned to sawdust as his menacing gaze met hers.

"Do as he says!" one of the men on the floor shouted at her.

Jennie eyed the door.

"Don't even think about it." The guard pushed her away from the door.

Jennie's gaze flitted between the two armed guards— one standing at the door and the other wheeling a cart stacked with canvas bags from the vault and weaving it around the bodies on the floor. The armed men weren't guards at all. They were bank robbers.

"On the floor." The man guarding the door took a step toward her. "I said, on the floor!"

Jennie dropped to her knees and flattened herself out on the gray Berber carpet.

"Stay where you are—all of you," he growled. "One move and I'll start shooting."

The man with the money threw the bags into the back of the armored truck—the one she'd parked beside.

Lisa is still in the car where the driver of the armored vehicle could see her. Oh, God, Jennie closed her eyes and offered up a fervent prayer. *This can't be happening. Please don't let them hurt Lisa. Please.*

Minutes dragged by like hours as the bank robber threw bag after bag of money into the back of the truck. Finally, with the last of the bags loaded, he jumped inside. "Let's get out of here."

His partner backed out, and with his gun still aimed at Jennie and the others, he let the glass doors swing shut.

Tires squealed as the driver peeled out.

With her heart still racing, Jennie got to her knees. She had to check on Lisa.

2

"Are you okay?" One of the men who'd been lying near her grasped her elbow and helped her up.

"Yeah." Jennie straightened her jean skirt and pink long-sleeved knit top. Her legs felt like cooked noodles.

The glass doors opened. Lisa stepped inside, her puzzled gaze flitting around the room and finally settling on Jennie. "What's wrong? What's going on?"

"We've just been robbed," answered the man who had helped Jennie up.

Jennie hurred to Lisa and hugged her. "I am so glad to see you. I thought maybe they'd taken you or something."

"Y-you mean like a bank robbery?" Lisa stammered. "But how? I was sitting right out there."

"They were using an armored truck—the one we parked next to." Jennie's voice sounded high and shaky.

"You're kidding, right?" Lisa bit into her lower lip and pressed folded arms against her stomach as if she were about to be sick. "So that guy who was flirting with me was a bank robber?" She grimaced and shook her hand in the air. "Yuck! He was staring at me. That's why I came inside. He was freaking me out."

"Well, at least you got a good look at him." Jennie's gaze swept past the others. None of them had been injured as she'd feared earlier. Though she'd been unharmed physically, Jennie felt dazed and disoriented. "Um . . . did someone call the police?"

"The alarm didn't work," the man who'd helped her said. "They must have somehow disarmed it. Randy's on the phone with a 9-1-1 operator now."

Randy must have been the woman in the glassed-in office on the far side of the room. She ran a hand down her blue flowered blouse and black slacks. Her still-frightened gaze darted around the room, settling on the pen she'd grabbed out of a black plastic holder on the desk.

"Don, could you give me a hand?" the second man asked. He was trying to assist a heavyset older woman with short, curly gray hair. The woman, wearing a tent-type dress, looked miserably uncomfortable in her attempts to get up. Both men strained to help her into a nearby chair.

Seeing the woman's open handbag and cane on the floor, Jennie hurried over to pick them up and stuffed the wallet and lipstick back inside the bag. She handed the purse and cane over to the woman, who appeared to be the only customer in the bank besides Jennie.

She thanked Jennie for retrieving the bag. "I can't believe this. Nearly had a heart attack. With all the bank robberies around here lately, you'd think the police would have an armed guard at every bank in Oregon."

"I'm sorry this had to happen while you were here, Mrs. Murray," Don said.

"No harm done." She heaved a sigh and leaned against her cane. "Now, if you'll help me out to my car . . ."

"I'm afraid I can't do that," he said. "You're a witness. We'll all have to wait here until the police come. Can I get you some coffee?"

"That would be nice, thank you." Mrs. Murray moaned as she adjusted her glasses and straightened her dress so that it covered her exposed knee.

Jennie wondered if she might be hurt more than she'd let on. "Do you need a doctor? We could call an ambulance."

"No, I'm fine. Knees and back are troubling me some. Not used to lying on floors, but at least it was carpeted." Mrs. Murray gave Jennie a trembling smile, then settled

11

back in the chair and began drinking her coffee. "What about you, honey? I was scared to death that monster was going to shoot you."

"Me too." Glancing at the clock on the wall, Jennie winced. Almost four. She was going to be late for the swim meet. DeeDee, her coach, would kill her. *"No excuses, Jennie,"* DeeDee had told her the last time she'd been late. *"Next time, you're off the team."* Jennie wondered if being caught in the middle of a bank robbery was a good enough reason to miss. Maybe if she called . . .

Jennie asked if she could use the phone and explained why. Don led her back to his office and turned the phone around. "Police ought to be here any minute."

"You're where?" DeeDee asked after Jennie explained that she'd be late. DeeDee didn't sound too pleased. "Let me get this straight. You were at a bank when it got held up? Jennie McGrady, I thought I'd heard them all, but that's the lamest excuse I've ever heard."

"It's true. Listen, I have to go. The police are just pulling in. Oh, and, DeeDee, please don't say anything to my mom and dad. They'll freak. I'm fine, and I'll tell them about it after the meet." Mom would be doubly upset when she heard the deposit had been in the car most of the day.

"I doubt I'll have time to talk to them anyway," DeeDee told her. "Just get here as soon as you can."

"Right." Jennie hung up and directed her attention to the police cars pulling into the parking lot.

An hour later Jennie entered Trinity High's gymnasium and headed for the lockers. Lisa went to join the spectators on the bleachers. On the way over, both girls decided the best way to handle matters was to let their parents know immediately, before they heard about it on the news. Lisa had promised to break the news to the family as gently as possible—especially to Jennie's mom, who was pregnant and tended to get rather emotional about things. At least

Jennie had made the deposit—even if it was a few hours late.

Jennie got undressed, showered, and shrugged into her suit in record time. She hoped she'd be able to move that fast in the pool, where it counted. There hadn't been time to prepare herself as she usually did with warm-ups and a pep talk from the coach. Still, if she concentrated, Jennie felt she could do a good job.

The once warm water from her shower now felt like ice chips on her skin. Toweling down, she slipped into her sweats and hurried to the poolside to check in with DeeDee.

"Are you sure you're up to this, Jennie? I heard about the robbery on the radio. Sorry I doubted you."

"I'll be okay." *For now, anyway.* She glanced toward the stands where Lisa was gesturing wildly. At least Mom didn't look mad . . . yet.

"Well, do some stretches to loosen up. You'll be on after the men's butterfly."

Jennie raised her arms and linked them above her head, stretching toward the ceiling. Five guys lined the end of the pool nearest her, then stepped up on the blocks. At the sound of the gun, they dove in. Kids and parents filling the bleachers yelled for their favorites.

Jennie shook out her hands and arms and moved her shoulders up and down. She was tight. And no wonder. Visions of the robbery played through her mind again. She'd given the officers as much information as she could, but it hadn't been enough. All she remembered was that both men had been thin, but barrel-chested from what she suspected were bullet-resistant vests. Their features had been hidden behind facial hair. Both had full mustaches and beards. She'd briefly seen the driver when she'd gone into the bank but couldn't describe him at all. She'd hoped Lisa would fill in the blanks on him, but she hadn't remembered much either, only that he was kind of cute and had light brown hair. He, too, had a mustache.

Things had happened so fast—too many details. *Relax,*

McGrady. It will come to you eventually. At least that's what Gram would have said. Gram knew about things like that. As far as Jennie was concerned, her grandmother, Helen Bradley, knew just about everything. Gram was a retired police officer and now worked as a travel writer. On occasion, she still did work as an undercover agent for the federal government.

Jennie jumped as firm hands settled onto her shoulders and began massaging. "Can't let you out of our sight for a minute, can we?"

"Hi, Dad." Jennie didn't turn around. She just hung her head while her father worked at the muscles in her neck. "What are you doing here?"

"I told you I'd try to come to all your meets."

"Yeah, but you've been so busy lately." Her father, Jason McGrady, was a homicide detective for the Portland Police Bureau.

"When am I not?" His voice was deep and soothing. Jennie felt herself relax a little.

"Lisa told you about the bank robbery?" Jennie groaned as he paused to rub an especially sore spot.

"Rocky told me before I came."

"How did he find out? He wasn't there." Rocky—Dean Rockwell—was a police officer and a good friend. He'd recently suffered a gunshot wound, and though he considered himself fit and ready for work, his boss insisted he take a full six weeks to recover. "He isn't back to work yet, is he?"

"No. He was at the office trying to convince the chief to let him come back to work. Poor guy—hates being out of the loop. Anyway, he heard the call come in. When he heard you were one of the witnesses, he called me."

Jennie sighed. "I shouldn't have been there. I was supposed to make the deposit this morning."

"I know. Lisa told us what happened."

"Is Mom mad at me?"

"What do you think?"

"I'm in trouble, huh?"

"A little. But we'll talk about that later. What matters is that you're safe." He reached around to give her a hug.

Jennie shrugged her shoulders and stepped away, embarrassed that the other kids might see her dad's open display of affection. No one seemed to notice except her mother. Susan McGrady was sitting on the lowest bench wearing a what-am-I-going-to-do-with-you look. Nick, Jennie's five-year-old brother, yelled something and waved.

Jennie waved back, then turned to face Dad. "Did they get the bank robbers yet?"

"No, but I'm sure they will." His dark blue gaze met hers. "You sure you're up to swimming?"

"Yeah. It'll help, Dad."

"Okay." He paused, looking as though he wanted to say more, then patted her shoulder. "Good luck."

She could hardly hear him over the cheers for the winner of the men's event.

"You're up, Jennie." DeeDee gave Dad a quick smile. Turning back to Jennie, she asked, "Everything all right?"

Jennie nodded, wishing everyone would stop asking her that. What was she supposed to say? "No, I'm not all right. My stomach is still rolling and pitching like a carnival ride. I can't stop thinking about what might have happened to Lisa if—"

DeeDee slapped her on the shoulder. "Go out there and win it for us, Jennie."

———

Jennie didn't win. She hadn't even come close. After the meet, DeeDee and her classmates gave her understanding hugs and encouragement, telling her it would be better next time.

"If I'd been through a robbery, I probably wouldn't have even tried," DeeDee said. "You gave it your best shot."

"Hey, Jen." With his camera perched on his shoulder, Gavin elbowed his way through the crowd. "Lisa, get next to her so I can get a shot of both of you." Gavin edited the school newspaper and worked as a stringer for the *Oregonian*, the area's primary newspaper.

Jennie groaned and gave him a murderous look. He knew how she hated publicity. She'd had way more than her share, but she pushed her still-wet hair straight back, hooked an arm around Lisa, and smiled. She'd learned one thing about Gavin: He'd take the shot and print it whether she wanted him to or not. The last time she'd objected, he'd caught her in the worst possible pose. She'd had her goggles on and looked like a wild-eyed fish.

Despite his persistence in getting the news and taking advantage of every photo opportunity, Gavin had become one of her best friends.

"Can you give me a lift to the newspaper office?" Gavin asked.

"I told him you would." Lisa beamed up at him. "He's going to write an article on the robbery."

"I'll need to check with Mom and Dad."

"I already did. We'll drop Gavin off and meet our parents at Giovanni's Pizza."

Four hours later Jennie sat in the living room watching the ten-o'clock news. The police still had not caught the bank robbers, who had somehow confiscated an armored car. So far there'd been no trace of the car or the real guards.

"I should have gone after them," Jennie muttered.

"No, you shouldn't have."

Jennie jumped, unaware she'd spoken aloud until her father rebuffed her.

Dad was sitting on the sofa cradling Mom's head. She'd fallen asleep an hour earlier and groaned softly when he spoke. "And don't be getting any ideas about getting involved in the investigation."

"I'm not."

"Now, why don't I believe that?" Dad stroked Mom's hair in a loving gesture that would have made Jennie smile under normal circumstances.

"Dad, I know how dangerous these guys are. It's just

that . . . I don't know. It makes me so mad. I just walked into the bank and stood there like a dummy. I can't even remember anything about them. I mean, how many guys in this town are thin and have beards and mustaches?"

Dad gave her a crooked smile, making the scar on his jaw stand out. "My guess is that all that facial hair is as phony as the uniforms."

Jennie stared at the television screen, processing her father's remark. Don, the bank manager, was being interviewed. "We had no clue," Don said. "These two guards walked in, and all of a sudden they pulled their guns and ordered us to the floor. I told everyone to comply. You don't want to antagonize these guys."

Jennie tuned him out. She'd already heard the story and doubted he'd come up with anything new. "You know, Dad, you might be right. I couldn't see the one guy very well, but the one holding his gun on everybody was only a few feet away. There was something really weird about him."

"Don't worry about it, princess. You did the best you could." He gently lifted his wife's head up and wrapped his arms around her. "Time for bed, honey. Want me to carry you up?"

Mom moaned and yawned. "S'all right," she mumbled. "I can walk."

Groggy from sleep, Mom hugged Jennie good-night, then turned back to Dad. The two of them made their way through the entry and up the stairs.

Dad turned back at the landing. "Go on up to bed, Jennie. I'll come back down and lock up."

"I can do it." Jennie pushed herself out of the chair and clicked off the television set. "I want to get a glass of milk anyway."

"All right, just don't stay up too late."

"I won't. Have to get up early tomorrow for our hike up at Lewis River."

"Looks like you'll have good weather for it."

"Hope so. Night, Dad. Night, Mom."

They mumbled their good-nights, and a few minutes later Jennie could hear them moving around in their bedroom above the kitchen. A comforting sound, she decided.

The excitement of the afternoon robbery and disappointment over her performance at the swim meet faded as she set about doing normal things, like opening the refrigerator and eating a leftover piece of chicken and pouring herself a glass of milk.

At eleven, Jennie made the final entry in the journal she kept in her bedside stand and turned out the lights. She'd written down everything she could remember about the robbery in her journal. Maybe tomorrow she'd be able to add more.

Jennie forced the robbery out of her mind by thinking about the great time she and Lisa and Scott and Gavin were going to have on their hike. Soon sleep came, and the brutal bank robbers seemed like remnants of a bad dream.

3

"Oh, that's too bad," Susan McGrady said into the cordless phone as she placed a carton of milk on the counter and reached into the cupboard for two glasses. "No, I understand."

Jennie wondered what disappointing news her mother had just received. It couldn't have been too catastrophic or Mom would be pacing the floor.

Jennie pulled the last of the waffles from the waffle iron and set it on the stack she'd just retrieved from the oven. She frowned and hoped Mom's telephone conversation didn't have anything to do with the hiking trip. Had Mom decided to punish her for not making the deposit on time and being at the bank when it got robbed? Jennie didn't think so. The night before, Mom had forgiven all. She'd been upset, but Dad had reminded her that the robbery could just as easily have taken place earlier in the day.

"Who is it?" Jennie asked.

Mom shook her head, gave her an I'll-tell-you-later look, then turned her attention back to the caller.

Annoyance with a small dose of worry crept in and settled in the pit of Jennie's stomach. It had taken her two days to get her parents to say yes to her and Lisa's hiking trip, and Jennie didn't want anything to spoil it. Scott, who claimed to be Jennie's boyfriend when he wasn't saving the environment, was already on his way.

So far everything was a go, including the weather. The

night before, the weather forecast for the Portland/Vancouver area had been for sunshine with scattered showers over the next few days. Now, at seven A.M., the early morning sun poured into the east windows, promising a clear and perfect day.

"Uh-huh." Mom kept the phone cradled between her ear and shoulder while she set the milk on the table and sat down. She mouthed to Jennie, "Get the orange juice."

Jennie grumbled and set the waffles down a little harder than she needed to.

Mom cast her a disparaging look.

"Sorry." Jennie was overreacting and she knew it. She hated being left out of things—like one-way conversations. *Face it, McGrady,* she told herself, *you're a first-class snoop.* Not that being nosy was all bad. Considering that someday she intended to go into law enforcement, Jennie usually regarded her nosiness as an admirable trait—one she shared with her dad and grandparents. She still wished she could have done something to deter the bank robbers. She imagined herself ignoring their threats and tackling the one with the gun. Why couldn't she have had more courage? Even though her father had told her she'd done the right thing by not going after them, Jennie felt certain that if she'd been fast enough, she'd have been able to follow them and let the police know where they were. On the other hand, there was a certain amount of common sense in what Dad had said. *"No amount of money is worth risking your life over."* Jennie believed that. But she still couldn't help wondering what would have happened if she'd been able to assess the situation more quickly and run for help.

You'd probably be dead, she reminded herself. That very sobering thought put an end to her *what if*s and *if only*s. At least for the moment.

Retrieving the juice, she rejoined her brother and mother at the table. Mom still clutched the phone in one hand while eating a piece of bacon with the other. "Mmm. No, I understand," she told the caller. "Hang on a sec. . . ."

Covering the mouthpiece she said, "Jennie, fix Nick's waffle for him, please."

Jennie, get the juice. Jennie, fix Nick's waffle. Jennie, do this. Jennie, do that. She was beginning to feel like Cinderella. Well, not exactly. Jennie reminded herself that her mother was, after all, pregnant and that she'd better not be too disagreeable lest she lose certain privileges, such as going hiking today. She put on a smile and said, "No problem."

Nick hardly seemed to notice as Jennie spread peanut butter on his waffle and folded it over. She smiled at his serious attempt to read the section of newspaper Dad had left on the table.

"What's those words?" Nick pointed to a headline that read *Bank Robbers Still At Large.*

Jennie read the headline and scanned the article. There had been a rash of robberies over the past month in the Portland/Vancouver area. The one involving Jennie was the first one where an armored car had been used. Jennie wondered if some or all of them might be connected. Authorities had been wondering the same thing, but they hadn't found any evidence linking them together. And they were no closer to catching any of the thieves involved.

Jennie stopped reading and tuned back in to her mother's conversation.

"I'd offer to take them," Mom said, "but Jason is working and Jennie will be gone all day."

"Who is it?" Jennie mouthed again.

This time Mom answered. "Emmie Morgan. Her car won't start."

Jennie groaned. She should have guessed. Andy's mom had a tendency to take ten minutes to explain what anyone else could in two. Of course, not having her car start would be a major problem, especially this morning. "Are they calling off the party?"

Nick's head jerked up. "What party? It better not be Andy's, 'cause Kurt and him and me are goin' camping for real."

"Andy's mom is on the phone," Jennie reiterated. "Her car won't start." Nick and Kurt, Lisa's little brother, had been invited to stay overnight at the Morgan home to celebrate Andy's seventh birthday.

Nick's blue eyes clouded as elephant tears formed and dripped onto his flushed cheeks. "So she can't come get us? And we can't go to Andy's birthday?"

"I don't know." Jennie shrugged and hurriedly added, "But don't worry. They'll think of something. Maybe Aunt Kate can take you."

Nick shook his head. "She's gotta work today, and Uncle Kevin is flying to California." Nick wiped his tears away with his shirt sleeve and popped a piece of waffle into his mouth. "You could take us. . . ."

"Sorry, little guy. I'm going hiking, remember?" Jennie's heart fluttered with renewed excitement and a hint of trepidation. She'd awakened with one of those odd feelings—like the kind she got before something really awful happened. She'd had the same feeling the day before but had attributed it to the fact that she'd forgotten to make the deposit. True, she'd been anxious about the money, but now she realized that her intuition must have been warning her about the bank robbery. The feeling flitted through her again, unsettling her stomach and taking away her appetite.

Nothing is going to happen, she assured herself. Aloud, as if to make it fact, she said, "Scott's coming here, and we're going to pick up Lisa and Gavin."

"Why can't you take me? You told me you were gonna be close to where Andy lives."

"We are." Jennie hugged him. She'd told him that to reassure him. This was his first camp-out without his family, and last night he'd been nervous about being away from home. "I'd be happy to take you, Nick, but there's no room in the car."

"We could sit on your laps."

"What about Bernie?" Bernie was the nearly full-grown Saint Bernard pup Kurt and Nick shared. "Trust me, Nick. There's no way you and Kurt and Bernie *and* your sleeping bags and clothes will fit into my car."

"I hate to disappoint the boys like this," Jennie heard her mother say. "But let's not give up yet. I have an idea. I'll talk to Jennie and call you back."

Jennie's stomach sank to the vicinity of her feet. Judging from the determined look on her mother's face, she had a feeling her perfect plans were about to be flushed right down the sewer.

4

"I know what you're thinking, Mom, and the answer is no." Jennie took a bite of waffle and didn't even taste it.

"Jennie." Mom shot her a warning look as she pulled out a chair and sat down. "You haven't heard my idea yet."

"I don't need to. You want me to drive them."

"It's the only logical solution."

"But, Mom," Jennie whined, "I can't back out of our trip. Scott will be here at nine. Lisa and Gavin are depending on me."

"I'm not asking you to give up your plans. Just alter them a little. You can drive the boys out to Battleground and meet your friends at the trailhead."

"But how are they going to get out there? Gavin doesn't drive, and Scott's car isn't big enough."

"Lisa can drive—of course, we'd have to clear it with Kate, but—"

"Lisa's grounded from driving until she passes the safety course. Besides, Aunt Kate wouldn't let her drive that far. Can't someone else take the boys? Maybe you could borrow Aunt Kate's car."

"I wish I could, honey." Mom sighed, patting her slightly rounded tummy. "It's too long a drive. My ankles are already swollen this morning and—"

"I know . . . I shouldn't have asked. But it isn't fair!"

"You know what the doctor said. Bed rest for two weeks and reduced activity. Drastically reduced. He's really concerned about the bleeding and . . . I can't take any chances." Mom grimaced. "I don't like this any more than you do, but if Nick doesn't go, you'll have to forget about the hiking trip altogether. I'll need you here to take care of him. Maybe we can pay for baby-sitting. I know you've been doing a lot of it lately."

"I don't care about the money, Mom. I love Nick, and most of the time I'm happy to take care of him. But it's just so exasperating. If things don't work out, it's always my plans that get axed. All I wanted was this one day with my friends, and it's getting totally messed up. I know I agreed to help out around here, but don't I count for something?" Jennie paused. "I don't mean to sound selfish, but sometimes I feel like what I want to do doesn't matter to you at all."

"I'm sorry, Jennie. I really am." She smiled. "But look on the bright side. The longest pregnancy is nine and a half months and we're nearly halfway there."

"Please, Jennie," Nick pleaded. "Please take me."

Jennie pressed her lips together. She'd probably already said too much, but it was so unfair. She put her fingers to work gathering up table crumbs and sweeping them into a pile. She mentally counted down from ten to one. *Four. It won't be that bad,* she told herself. *Three. It's not like you can't go at all. Two . . .*

"Jennie." Nick squeezed between the chair and table and crawled into her lap. Wrapping his arms around her neck, he peered directly into her eyes. "You're gonna take us, right?"

Jennie couldn't help but smile. Her brother had a terminal case of the cutes. "Yeah." She rubbed his head, mussing up his dark, thick hair. His grip around her neck tightened. "I wouldn't want you to miss your first real camp-out." She'd find a way. Maybe if she, Lisa, and Mom joined forces, Aunt Kate would relent and let Lisa drive. Otherwise she'd just come back and they'd go hiking somewhere closer.

"Yes!" He scrambled down and ran out of the room.

"Nick," Mom called after him, "come back here and finish your breakfast." Running a hand through her disheveled auburn hair, Mom gave Jennie a warm smile.

"Thanks, honey. I knew I could count on you."

"Yeah, right."

Someone knocked on the back door, then opened it. "Hey, just me." Aunt Kate swooped into the kitchen. Kurt zipped around her, gave Nick a high-five, and the two of them shot off to Nick's room.

"Honestly," Mom grinned after them. "All this excitement over a backyard camp-out."

"This is a big deal for all the boys." Kate gave Jennie and Mom quick hugs, then headed for the coffeepot. "They will be out in the country. Lots of woods around the Morgan place. Remember our first camping trip, Susie? *Before* we had all these kids?"

Mom laughed. "How could I forget? That female cougar screaming in the middle of the night." She made a face and shuddered. "Scared me half to death. I thought some woman was being killed."

Kate poured herself a cup of coffee and sat at the table across from Mom. "That was scary. But what really had me worried was the coyotes. I thought for sure they were going to come right into our tents and devour us."

"And what a big help our husbands were!" Mom laughed at the memory. "Remember how Jason and Kevin decided to go outside the tent to make sure we were safe?"

Kate smiled. "Right, then they started hitting the tent and clawing at the canvas, making like bears."

"I hope an adult will be staying outside with Nick and Kurt." Jennie was well aware of the animal sounds in the woods at night. She remembered all too clearly the time she'd been lost. Not for long, thank goodness, but long enough to get good and scared.

"Oh, no need to worry, Jennie," Mom said. "Jim and Emmie will keep a close eye on them. I think Andy's older brother . . . What's his name again?"

"Jeremiah," Jennie responded.

"Right." Mom picked up her sentence again. "Jeremiah will be staying out with them."

"Now, that's comforting." Jennie knew the guy from

church, which is where their families had met. Jeremiah was Jennie's age and a big tease. He'd probably do his best to entertain the boys with all sorts of scary stories.

"Relax, hon," Kate said. "Nick will be fine."

"I suppose," Jennie sighed. "I guess I'd better call Lisa."

"Call Lisa about what?" Kate asked.

Mom filled her in on the change of plans.

While Mom and Kate talked, Jennie let her gaze drift from her aunt to her mother. They were so totally different. Both pretty. Mom was short—almost a head shorter than Kate—with shoulder-length auburn hair that curled naturally in all the right places. Mom looked a lot like Lisa. Jennie, on the other hand, being as tall as Kate with the same dark hair and eyes, looked like she could have been Kate's daughter.

No wonder a lot of people got confused as to which kids belonged with whom. Uncle Kevin, Kate's husband, was Mom's brother. And to make matters even more complicated, Jennie's dad was Kate's twin brother. What a tangle.

"At any rate," Mom was saying when Jennie tuned back in, "everything should work out okay as long as you don't mind Lisa driving out there."

Kate sipped at her coffee, then glanced from Jennie to Susan. "I don't know. It's quite a ways—like sixty miles or something, isn't it?"

"I'll understand if you don't want her to," Mom said. "Especially after that speeding ticket she got last month."

Jennie held her breath.

Looking pensive, Aunt Kate took a sip of her coffee. "And I suppose Jason is working today?"

Mom nodded. "With all the robberies, they've been shifting people around. Jason lost a couple of officers that normally work Homicide. And until they make some solid arrests . . ." Mom took a deep breath. "Okay, listen. I agree it's a long drive on narrow, windy roads. If you'd rather she didn't, maybe Jennie can take the boys out and drive back here to pick up the others. It would shorten their hiking by a couple of hours, but . . ."

Kate shook her head. "I couldn't do that to the girls. Not with Scott coming all the way in from Newport. I'm sure Lisa will do fine. She's improved a lot since she started the safety course. And she'll have another licensed driver with her. Scott does drive, doesn't he?"

"Yes!" Jennie bounced up and hugged her. "Thanks, Aunt Kate. You're the best."

"Either that or I get conned easily." Kate glanced at her watch and bolted to her feet. "Love to stay and chat, but I have to get going. I left Kurt's stuff on the porch." Kate grabbed one last swig of coffee and set the mug in the sink. "Susie, if you need anything, call me."

"A lot of good that will do. You won't have a car."

"No, but I have a phone, and the pastor gave me a list of people from Trinity who are willing to help out. See you." Aunt Kate swooped out as she had swooped in—in a rush.

The minute Kate left, Jennie sent her mom to her room to rest. She smiled. It felt good to be able to give direction rather than take it for a change. Mom didn't even argue, and that worried Jennie a little. As she tidied the kitchen, she grabbed the cordless phone and punched in Lisa's number.

Jennie tried to explain the situation quickly but had only gotten to the part about having to take the boys to Battleground when Lisa cut in.

"I can't believe your mom could be so mean," Lisa complained. "It isn't fair. We've been planning this trip forever."

Jennie dug into the refrigerator for sandwich fixings. "She isn't being mean, Lisa. It really isn't anyone's fault that Mrs. Morgan's car broke down. Anyway, it's not so bad. Your mom is going to let you drive the guys out there. You'll have to pick up Gavin, then stop by here to get Scott."

"You're kidding," Lisa squealed. "She's actually letting me drive? Cool." Jennie imagined Lisa's freckled face splitting into a wide grin. "Hey, Mom bought us this great trail mix with dried bananas and chocolate chips and nuts. Are the sandwiches ready?"

"I'm working on them."

"Great. I have the chips and drinks all packed." She

sighed. "I can hardly wait to get started. What time should we plan on meeting you and where?"

"I should be able to get to the Lower Falls Campground by nine. We can pick up the trail there. I have to leave here at eight to take the boys, so that will be just about right."

"Sounds good," Lisa said. "I'm so excited. So is Gavin. I talked to him last night." And off she went. Lisa could talk for hours about how Gavin Winslow was the neatest guy she'd ever dated. Jennie was happy to see the two of them together. Gavin really was a great guy. Extremely intelligent. He'd liked Lisa for quite a while but didn't think she'd be interested in a tall, skinny guy who wore glasses and wanted to be a news anchor instead of a sports hero. This past summer he would have been right. Lisa's idea of a dream date had been built like a football player. She'd changed a lot since then.

Jennie cut Lisa's monologue short with, "We'd better finish getting ready."

"Right. I still have to shower and get dressed. See you soon."

Jennie punched the Off button and set the phone on the counter. While she concentrated on making sandwiches, a sense of foreboding rose from her stomach and clogged her throat. She hated the feeling because she never knew exactly what would happen or when. Like with the bank robbery the day before.

Gram had told her that sometimes all you can do is pray and try to cover the bases. "God," Jennie mumbled, "don't let anything bad happen. Protect Lisa and make her drive safely. Please let us have a good day." Jennie added prayers for her parents and the boys, pushing away her negative feelings.

She determined that this was going to be a good day. "Make that a *great* day!"

5

"What a perfect day!" Jennie slid behind the wheel and watched her mom bestow final hugs and kisses on both boys. The kids tumbled into the car, noisy and bouncy. Jennie almost felt like a chauffeur with the boys insisting on sitting together in the backseat. Bernie, the massive pup, started out in back, but as soon as Jennie started backing out, he climbed into the front—not to keep her company, Jennie noted ruefully, but to get some rest. He curled up on the seat and closed his eyes.

On the way out to the farm, Jennie turned the radio on to one of her favorite stations. As she sang along, she thought of Ryan and Scott and wondered why. Not difficult to figure out, she supposed. Not when she allowed herself to think honestly about the two guys she'd sort of considered her boyfriends.

Ryan Johnson was gorgeous, blond, slightly taller than Jennie. They'd been friends for years, and since he lived next to her grandmother at the coast, she'd practically grown up with him. Every time she went to visit Gram—Dad and Aunt Kate's mother—they hung out together. Last summer they'd become a little more than friends, but then he decided he wanted to go out with another girl. So they were back to the friend stage.

Scott, on the other hand, seemed very interested in her. Her only competition so far was his insistence on saving the environment single-handedly. She shared his views on most environmental issues and understood his desire to get a degree in marine biology. In fact, it was his dedication that she liked most about him. But sometimes he was just too intense.

Not that she didn't like intense. She just wasn't ready for a serious relationship. Still, she had to admit he was pretty cute. Scott had dark hair and green eyes that reminded Jennie of the brilliant waters surrounding the island where they'd first met. Miracle Key. Jennie smiled. They were both a little hotheaded at the time. She thought he'd acted like a total jerk, but even then she couldn't deny her attraction to him. They'd become friends over the next couple of weeks. And when he came out west to pursue his studies, they'd connected again. In some ways Jennie liked that connection. In other ways he made her a little nervous and she wasn't sure why.

"When are we gonna be there?" Nick asked.

Jennie reined in her thoughts and focused on her surroundings. "Soon, Nick. See where that red light is down there? That's Battleground. We're supposed to turn there and head for the Lewis River." She checked her directions again.

"But how long?"

"He has to go to the bathroom, Jennie," Kurt said. "I do too."

"Um . . . we should be there in ten minutes. Can you wait that long?"

"I guess." Kurt settled back against the seat.

"Me too," Nick mimicked.

They made it in ten. The Morgans' big new house sat on a hillside surrounded by acres of pastureland and trees. Two chestnut horses nibbled casually at the grass in the fenced-in pasture.

Kurt and Nick tumbled out of the car and took off running toward the porch. Their buddy Andy bounded down the stairs. Bernie, still sleepy from the drive, ambled behind, not sure what to make of things. Two overly friendly golden retrievers raced around the corner to meet them.

They seemed as eager to see Bernie as Andy was to see the boys.

"Hey, Jennie!" Jeremiah came up behind her and poked her in the ribs. "You staying over too?"

She jumped, then turned around and slugged him in the arm. "No."

"Ouch." He winced, feigning serious pain.

"Come off it. That didn't hurt."

"Did too. You're pretty strong for a girl."

"Thanks." Jennie grinned.

He returned the smile, his brown eyes softening. Running a hand though his short, curly blond hair, he said, "Sure you don't want to stay?"

"Sorry. I have other plans."

He pretended to pout. "My heart is broken."

"Sure it is."

He put a hand to his heart. "I'm serious. I'd really like you to hang around."

"I'm sure you would. Let me guess. You're stuck taking care of the boys tonight and want someone your own age to talk to."

He grimaced. "You got that right."

Jennie's smile widened. "I'm sure you'll have a great time. Roasting marshmallows and—"

"Telling ghost stories?" He raised his eyebrows.

"Jeremiah!" Jennie turned serious. "About that. Nick's pretty small. I'd appreciate it if you went easy on him. I'd hate to have to drive clear out here tonight to pick him up."

His gaze met hers, and Jennie had the oddest feeling he wouldn't mind a bit if she had to come back. He must have felt it, too, as his playful attitude quickly changed. "Sure. I was only teasing. I'll make sure he doesn't get scared."

"Thanks." She flashed him another smile and grabbed Nick's sleeping bag out of the car.

"Here." Jeremiah wedged himself in beside her. "Let me give you a hand."

Fifteen minutes later, Jennie set off to rendezvous with her friends. She was excited about seeing Scott again. On the other hand, she felt uncomfortable not knowing how she really felt about him. Or about Ryan. If she ever had to choose between them, Jennie honestly didn't know whom she'd pick. Not wanting to think about it, Jennie bumped up the volume on the radio. Being out in the country made the signal weaker. Before long she lost it altogether and tried another station.

"Police are still looking for the three men who held up the Lake Oswego Branch of the U.S. National Bank yesterday afternoon. Early this morning the Clark County Sheriff's Department reported finding the stolen armored truck used in the robbery. They're narrowing their search to the Vancouver area."

"Good," Jennie said aloud.

"Vancouver police have a make on a vehicle that may be the getaway car. A gray '85 Chevy Cavalier. Rust spots on the rear end. Washington plates *AXY 850*. Anyone with information is asked to call their local law enforcement agency immediately. Suspects are considered armed and dangerous."

A cold chill shuddered through her. She glanced into her rearview mirror. *Relax, McGrady. There isn't a car in sight. You couldn't be safer.* But Jennie wasn't so sure. That foreboding feeling she'd had earlier returned. Her intuition was definitely warning her about something.

Jennie again told herself she had nothing to worry about. Vancouver was miles away. The bank robbery had taken place yesterday in Portland. The men would be long gone by now.

Maybe what her intuition was telling her had nothing to do with the bank robberies. Maybe her intuition was warning her about the hiking trip—telling her to go back home. That they might encounter some sort of danger along the trail.

Jennie shook her head. "No way am I going back now. I promised Lisa I'd meet them here, and that's exactly what I'm going to do." If she still felt uncomfortable about the hike when they arrived, she'd talk to them about going somewhere else.

The farther she drove into the mountains, the more her anxiety heightened. Jennie scrutinized each car she saw. Several were older models, but none matched the description the disc jockey had given.

"You're imagining things, McGrady," she muttered to herself. "You're spooked."

She passed several logging trails that left the main highway. Each time she did, she imagined the trail leading to a hideout. She wondered what she'd do if she did spot the car. Follow it? No, that would be too risky. She'd go to the nearest town and use a pay phone to call the sheriff. Jennie chided herself again for letting her imagination run away with her. There was no reason to think the robbers would be hiding out here.

By the time she reached the Lewis River Falls area, Jennie had put the bank robbers out of her mind. They were a world away in a city of asphalt and steel. She had entered a pristine forest—a God-shaped world with blue skies above and trees as old as time surrounding her.

Jennie drove into the wooded area and parked near the trail. There were no other cars. Disappointment filled her. Though she didn't really expect them yet, she had hoped Lisa and the guys would be waiting. She glanced at her watch and groaned. Jennie was ten minutes early, and knowing Lisa, she'd be at least ten minutes late.

A trio of Steller's jays scolded raucously from somewhere in the forest's overstory. Jennie wondered what they were complaining about. Maybe they were upset with her for invading their quiet home.

Rolling down the window, she leaned back and drew in a long, deep breath of fresh mountain air. Closing her eyes, she cherished the cool breeze floating over her face. She listened to Celine Dion sing a beautiful love song. Instead of thinking about Ryan and Scott, Jennie thought of the numerous times she'd helped the police bring a criminal to justice. She had a few years to go, but soon she'd be out of high school, pursuing her law degree. Then she'd be in a position to go after criminals like—

The crunch of footsteps on gravel jerked Jennie out of her reverie. The hairs on the back of her neck stiffened and stood at attention like armed guards. She glanced around quickly but saw no one. Her heart raced as she reached for her lock and pressed it. She rolled up the window on her side, then reached across the seat to do the same on the passenger side.

A man appeared at the window and ripped the door out of her hand. "Too late for that." A skinny, balding guy with graying hair slipped into the passenger seat. He offered her a sly grin.

Jennie grabbed for the lock beside her shoulder with her right hand and the door handle with her left.

She froze as she heard a distinctive *click* and spotted the gun in his hand.

"I wouldn't do that if I were you." He closed the door and ordered her to start the car.

"W-what if I refuse?" Jennie said with much more bravado than she felt.

"Then I'll have to shoot you."

Jennie's left hand still gripped the door handle. She'd managed to lift the lock. Maybe she could bolt out the door and run into the woods. Buy herself some time.

With her left hand secure on the handle, Jennie used her right to twist the key until the engine turned over. "Why don't you let me go. Y-you can take my car." Her voice was shakier now.

"And leave you behind to identify me? No way."

Jennie put the car in gear and took her foot off the brake. The car began to roll back. Jennie pulled the handle.

"Stay put!" He raised his gun and fired.

6

The wilderness swallowed up the explosion of the gunshot and Jennie's scream. The bullet whizzed past her kneecaps and thunked into the door near the handle.

Jennie snapped her hand back and grabbed the steering wheel as if it were a life preserver.

"Now drive." The man sneered. "I'm not into killing folks, but there's always a first time. If you behave yourself, you might just come out of this alive."

"Yeah," she muttered. "Like you're really going to let me go."

He shook his head. "Just my luck, I have to run into another mouthy teenager."

"I—"

"Just shut up and get moving."

Too scared to argue, Jennie backed the car around as slowly as she could manage without attracting the man's attention. Maybe someone would come along—a ranger or sheriff.

Please, God, she prayed. *Please let Lisa come.* As soon as the prayer formed in her mind, Jennie realized the danger her friends would be in if they did show up. The guy was armed.

Scratch that, Lord, she amended. *Please don't let them be in danger. Just help me get through this.*

Jennie had been in hostage situations before and always managed to get away. She just had to keep her cool and look for the best method of escape.

"Take a left," he ordered.

"Are you sure?" The question slipped out before Jennie could stop it. A left turn would take them back toward town, which was fine with Jennie. With any luck at all, they would meet Lisa, and she'd see that Jennie was in trouble and call the police.

"What are you, deaf or something?"

"No, but—"

"Then move." He jabbed the gun in her side. "No way am I leaving the loot in that piece of junk."

Piece of junk? As in car? It made sense now. He must have heard the same broadcast she had. He knew the police would be looking for his car. He'd had to ditch it and was hoping to pick up another one. It happened to be hers.

News of the bank robberies came on the radio again.

"Turn it up." He grinned, and Jennie noticed a missing molar. She also noticed a small scar on his left index finger and got a partial view of a tattoo on his sinewy deltoid.

"You're one of the bank robbers, aren't you?" She reached for the dial and increased the volume.

"Shut up. I want to hear this."

The disc jockey gave the same report he'd given earlier about the missing car. The announcer chuckled. "Between you and me, these guys aren't too bright. If I were out to steal a car, I'd go with something new and snazzy. Maybe a Jag . . ."

"A lot you know, smart face." He silenced the radio with a twist of the knob.

"Why didn't you steal a newer car?" Jennie asked.

"Why do you think?"

"So you wouldn't be noticed?"

"Give the girlie a prize. People don't notice older cars, and they're easy to hot-wire." He smiled again. "Went like clockwork. Don't know what went wrong. We checked out the owner like always. Didn't figure she'd miss it till she finished up work tonight. By then we'd have all been out at the cabin. Miserable piece of junk didn't even run good, but it had a full tank of gas."

"My car will be easier to spot," Jennie said. "I was supposed to meet my friends. When I'm not there they'll call the police. They'll send out helicopters and—"

"By that time this baby will be clean out of sight," he interrupted. "Too bad. It's a nice little car. Maybe we can switch plates and change the color." He rooted around in the glove box and pulled out the insurance card and registration. After scanning the forms, he peered at her over the top of them. "Let me guess. You're Jennie McGrady?"

Jennie didn't bother to deny it.

"Name's Jon," he offered.

Jennie didn't want to know his name. Didn't want to think about what knowing too much would mean for her.

"Slow down." He scanned the road and pointed to a blue plastic bag flapping against a small tree. "Take a left here," he ordered.

Jennie turned hard, slamming him against the door, hoping to knock him around and give herself time to escape. He didn't seem to notice.

"Where are we going?" Jennie's Mustang rode the bumpy, overgrown logging road like a cowboy on a bronc. She gripped the steering wheel as it whipped back and forth. Tree limbs crackled and scraped the sides of her car.

"Slow down!" Jon yelled.

About a quarter of a mile in, Jennie crunched to a stop just before the road dipped into a ravine. Below, under a canopy of vine maple and rotting leaves, she spotted the hidden car. He'd driven it down an embankment. No wonder he'd seemed so sure of himself; it would be years before anyone found it.

Jon ordered her out of the car and pushed her in front of him. When they reached the Chevy, he opened the trunk. Four big black garbage bags filled the space. Twenty-dollar bills spilled out of one. Using a twist tie, Jon quickly closed it up.

"Grab two and start moving."

Jon kept his gun trained on her while she carried and dragged the bags up the hill and stuffed them into the trunk of her car. Within minutes they'd returned to the main road, this time heading up the mountain, farther away from town. They passed the road to the campground where she was to have met Lisa, Scott, and Gavin. They would be there by now. Jennie imagined herself making a sharp right into the campground area. *Then what?* Her own voice of reason ridiculed the idea. She wouldn't make it more than a couple of yards before Jon shot her. And if her friends were there she'd put them in danger as well.

"You won't get away with this." Jennie glanced over at him and wished she hadn't.

He took direct aim at her. "Who's going to stop us? You?" He tipped his head back and laughed. "Listen, little girl, we've managed to sidestep the law in ten states, and we're about to make it eleven. So don't be getting any fancy ideas about stopping us."

As much as Jennie wanted to tear down his inflated ego and boast about the law enforcement agencies in the area, she didn't. No sense getting him mad. She'd bide her time until she got her bearings. What he didn't know was that Jennie had resources of her own. She was a cop's kid— strong and intelligent. Most importantly Jennie had no intention of giving up without a fight.

"Eleven states." Jennie pretended to be impressed by his success. "How did you manage that?"

He eyed her suspiciously for a moment, then went into a spiel about how easy it was to catch most bank robbers. "Anybody can rob a bank. But they get caught because they don't plan their getaway with enough detail. Maude and Junior and me . . . well, we got it down to a science."

"Really, how's that?"

"We've always got alternative plans. When problems come up, we got ways to circumvent them."

"I'm sure most bank robbers think they have it all figured out, too, but eventually—"

He cut her off with a sharp look. "They don't keep switching cars."

"What do you mean?"

"We switch getaway vehicles as much as two to three times a job. Sometimes we buy old clunkers for cash from private owners. Other times we just steal them. Never with people in them, of course. We don't like leaving witnesses behind."

"Then why didn't you just take my car and leave me behind?"

"You can ID me. I told you I'm not a killer. This here was an emergency. Wouldn't have been very neighborly of me to leave you stranded, now, would it?" He chuckled. "Not so close to the cabin, anyways. Don't want the police snooping around out here. I had planned on ditching that old dinosaur in another day or two anyway. This works out just as well. Lucky you happened along."

"Yeah, lucky. Then again, maybe not. The police are going to comb this entire mountain looking for me."

"It'll take a while for your friends to figure out you're missing and not just late. Or maybe they'll think you ran away. By the time they get to looking for you, both you and your car will have vanished."

"What are you going to do with me?"

He used the barrel of the gun to scratch his forehead. "Don't rightly know as yet. Have to see what Maude thinks about it. Chances are we'll just leave you at the cabin. Figure you can't get into too much trouble way out here."

Jennie's hopes soared.

"Or we could take you along as a hostage." He frowned. "Only that might draw too much attention to us. We wouldn't want that."

"No, you wouldn't."

"Now that I think about it, describing us to the police won't do you much good. We look pretty ordinary." He grinned at her again, letting the gun rest on his legs. "That's another thing we're good at. Every job, we wear different disguises."

Like the armed-guard uniforms and the beards they'd worn yesterday. The facial hair and bullet-resistant vest were gone, but Jennie thought he might have been the guy hauling the money out of the bank. She wondered if he recognized her. Must not have. Of course, he hadn't been looking at her either. But his partner had. Maude. But that was a woman's name.

Jennie suddenly realized what had been so odd about the guard who'd held them hostage. She'd assumed because of the facial hair it had been a man. Thinking back now, Jennie realized he must have been a she. Jennie kept her thoughts to herself. Hopefully he and his partners wouldn't realize she'd been a witness at yesterday's bank heist.

"Where are we headed?" Jennie asked.

"We got a cabin. We're good at that too—picking places to stay. Nice, cozy little spot. Off the beaten track. Owners obviously like their privacy. It's at least fifteen miles to the nearest neighbor."

Fifteen miles. It would be rough, but she could hike out. *Provided they let me go or I can escape.* She shoved aside the negative thought. "Owners? Is someone letting you borrow it?"

"In a manner of speaking." There was that sly grin again. "Belongs to some people in Vancouver. It's their summer cabin, but they won't be coming up for a while."

"How do you know that?"

"We checked the family out. Mrs. Graham is out of town until next week. Kids have some kind of outdoor survival thing going on next week. We'll be cleared out by then."

Graham. Jennie memorized the name. She'd have another piece of evidence to give the police.

Stupid, Jennie thought. *The guy is really stupid to give me so much information.* If she could keep him talking she'd know more than enough to help the police build a case against him and his creepy accomplices.

Be careful, McGrady, her voice of reason warned. *Don't*

underestimate him. He may not be as dumb as you think. Maybe he's telling you all this stuff because he doesn't plan on letting you live long enough to do anything with it.

On the other hand, maybe nothing he's telling you is true. He could be stringing you along. But what if he isn't? What if the time comes for them to leave, and he and Maude and Junior decide you know too much? What then?

7

"Pull in here," Jon directed. He pointed to a gravel road that cut a narrow path through the woods.

Jennie tried to find something that would serve as a reminder when she brought the police back here. There was nothing. No mailbox, downed tree stump—nothing except the one-lane road winding to who knew where. Jennie checked her speedometer. She'd driven 15.8 miles since leaving the trailhead to where the road began.

Fifteen point eight. She repeated the thought over and over like a litany.

Her abductor had been a little short in his estimation of the distance to the cabin, but he'd been right about the place being secluded. Jennie hadn't seen another car or sign of human habitation for miles. She still couldn't see this one. With every mile her anticipation grew. Never had she felt so alone and isolated. She had tried to memorize road signs and markings on the drive up and hoped she could find it on the map later. After she'd escaped.

If you escape. The thought twisted her insides, bringing on another wave of panic.

No, she couldn't let herself be afraid. She had to keep her wits about her. It was her only hope.

Five miles down the dusty road, the mountain cabin finally came into view.

Jennie had expected rustic, but this was far from it. The two-story cabin with dormers was nestled between towering firs, oak, and maples and had a fantastic view of a river—Jennie had no idea which river. The cabin seemed to have been recently built. A weekend getaway—a place to come and relax. A place she wouldn't mind visiting sometime, just not with a bank robber.

She drove in to the end of the road, which had been widened to fit several cars. There were two buildings besides the cabin. A small shed with a stained-glass window and another larger one. A shop, Jennie decided when she glanced through the open double doors and saw the stacks of lumber and tools lining one wall. A table saw sat in the center with piles of sawdust scattered across the concrete floor.

"Nice place, ain't it?"

"Yeah." Jennie gripped the steering wheel. With any luck at all the man would get out of the car and she could zip around and peel out of there. Unfortunately, he wasn't about to give her that chance.

He kept the gun trained on her as he prodded her out of the car and up the steps onto the wraparound porch. Reaching around her, he opened the door and gave her a shove from behind. "Have a seat. And don't get any ideas about taking off."

"Look," she said, trying to keep her voice as stable as possible, "I'm not stupid. I don't want to get shot, so why don't you just put the gun away."

He snorted. "You'd like that, wouldn't you?"

Jennie sank into a comfortable-looking sofa. The plush velour cushions rose around her. The people who owned this place had money, no doubt about that. She tipped her head back and closed her eyes. *What am I going to do, God? How am I going to get out of here?*

Opening her eyes, she let her gaze wander about the room, determined to look for escape routes. The cabin had a vaulted ceiling over the living room. The lower-ceilinged kitchen was roomy with lots of cupboard space. A table and four chairs sat beside two windows. Both had screens and looked as though they could be opened easily. There was a closed door off the living room, maybe a bedroom or bath-room. Next to it were stairs leading to the upper level. A sliding-glass door from the living room went out to the deck, which overlooked the river. The many windows and airiness of the cabin pushed away some of Jennie's fears and renewed her spirits. If he left her alone for a few min-utes, she could easily make her getaway. And once she did, she'd disappear into the woods and follow the river down the mountain.

"I need to use the bathroom." Jennie got up from the couch and took a step toward Jon. She wanted a closer look at the back part of the house. Maybe the bathroom would have a window.

He eyed her suspiciously. "Sure. No problem." He pointed the gun at the door. "It's outside."

Jennie wrinkled her nose. "Outside?"

"Yeah. Strange, huh? They built this modern cabin without an indoor bathroom."

Pushing Jennie ahead of him, Jon showed her around to the back of the cabin to a small square building with a round window in the door. The window, about two feet in diameter, was made of stained glass in a multicolored floral pattern. She stepped into the outhouse and locked it, then turned around and leaned against the door.

Relieved to be out of Jon's sight, Jennie began to relax. She felt a little like Alice in Wonderland, exploring a strange new world. The outhouse was like no other out-house she'd ever seen. The tiny room was equipped with all the modern fixtures you'd see in a regular bathroom. Toilet, sink, shower, and shelves for toiletries and towels. There were toothbrushes and toothpaste, along with some first-aid supplies in a basket under the counter. In one drawer she found a flashlight—probably for emergencies if the lights went out. She pushed on the end and smiled. The batteries were good. If she did manage to escape she might take it with her.

A light-and-fan fixture hung from the high ceiling, but the only window was the lovely stained glass. No way of escape. Not anxious to face her captor again, Jennie lowered the lid of the toilet and sat there a moment. The sunlight coming through the colored glass made rainbows on the walls and on her arms. A cocoon of safety.

"Hey, hurry up in there." Jon's threatening voice shattered the warm stillness.

"Coming." Jennie quickly used the facilities, washed up, and reluctantly stepped outside.

Instead of taking her back into the house, Jon stopped in front of a storage shed on the deck. Sliding back the bolt, he opened it and ordered Jennie to go inside.

"No, please . . ." When Jennie held back he shoved her into a stash of lawn chairs, bikes, games, balls, and camping gear.

"Shut up and do as you're told." Jon slammed the shed door behind her, plunging the cramped space into total darkness. " 'Bout time you learned some respect."

His footsteps faded. Tears stung Jennie's eyes as she untangled herself from the clutter. She rubbed at a painful spot where she'd scraped her forearm. She backed up until she hit the door, then slid to the floor and rested her arms on her knees. Even though being abducted was a horrible thing, she had a feeling deep in the pit of her stomach that the ordeal was far from over. After spending several minutes crying and berating herself for not listening to her intuition earlier, Jennie prayed.

Subdued light eventually seeped in through various cracks and knotholes in the unpainted wood. She had more space in which to move around than she'd originally thought. Pulling loose one of the chaise lounges, she opened it up and lowered herself into it. She had to think. What would her father or Gram do in a situation like this? They probably would have delivered a karate kick to the door and knocked Jon senseless.

Jennie sighed. She was strong, but not strong enough to overtake a grown man. She'd never taken karate. And she didn't have a clue as to how to escape. If he hadn't locked her in the storage shed . . .

Storage shed!

Tools.

Maybe if she quit feeling sorry for herself and dug through the collection of odds and ends the owners kept in the shed, she'd find something she could use to break out. If nothing else she could use a hammer or something to knock down the walls or hit her abductor over the head.

Jennie began a methodical search, mostly by feel. An hour later she sat back down in the chair. The small storage area was hot and stuffy. Twice during her search Jon had come outside and pounded on the wall, yelling at her to be quiet. That was hard to do when you had to work around two mountain bikes, a Weed Eater, a lawn mower, a volleyball and net, badminton birdies, a croquet set, garden hoses, garden tools, and who knew what else. She'd set the wooden mallet aside. It might work as a hammer. There were several potential weapons, including a sharp pair of pruning shears.

She heard the crunch of gravel as a car drove in. Jennie rose and peered through the knothole she'd found in the exterior wall.

"'Bout time you got here," Jon yelled from somewhere nearby. Jennie watched a woman in tight black jeans and a red-and-gray jacket emerge from a dusty blue car. She flicked ashes from her cigarette to the ground.

"Where'd you get those wheels?" she asked in a raspy voice as she pointed to Jennie's car. "Where's the one you had at the motel this morning?"

"Had to ditch it. Owner reported it missing. Heard on the radio coming up here that the police were lookin' for it. Man, nearly missed getting picked up too. Passed a trooper and thought I was a goner. Next thing I knew, this white Chrysler whipped into the left lane, going like his tail was on fire. Trooper tore out after him. Didn't want to take no more chances, so I dumped it."

"You didn't leave it along the side of the road, I hope?"

He shook his head. "'Course not, Maude. Found an

old logging road and drove in a ways. No way the cops are gonna find it."

"Where's the money?"

"Now, quit worrying, will ya?" He pointed to Jennie's car. "It's in the trunk."

"Where'd you find the Mustang?"

Jon told her how he'd left the car only a mile from the campground and how Jennie had obligingly let him have her vehicle.

"You brought the owner back here with you?" The woman swore and stomped up the steps. "What were you thinking?"

"Didn't have much choice. Just cool down and let me explain. This was the only vehicle around, and she was waitin' on some friends. Couldn't very well leave her there to tell the cops. As it is, I bought us time to get rid of the Mustang before the cops start searching for her."

"Well, that's just fine and dandy." Maude tossed the cigarette butt on the driveway and put her hands on her hips.

"Now, Maude, just calm yourself down. The kid won't be any trouble. I got her locked in the storage shed."

"What do you plan to do with her while we're gone? Anybody with an ounce of brains could get out of there in five seconds flat. In case you've forgotten, that's where the owners of this place keep their tools."

Jon looked like he was about to slug her. "I wasn't planning to leave her in the storage shed for long. Just got tired of watching her."

"Where's Junior?"

Jon shrugged. "Thought he was with you. I been here over two hours waitin' for you to show up. What took you so long?"

"I went east along the gorge like we'd planned and came up through Carson. Hit some construction work on the Washington side. Not sure what happened to Junior. He left the motel before I did this morning. Should have been here by now."

"On the way up I heard the police had a suspect. You don't suppose. . . ?"

"The only way they'da gotten Junior is if he walked up to them and turned himself in."

"Hope you're right. Don't know if the boy has it in him to get through an interrogation without cracking." He raised a fist. "I tell you, Maude, if that boy ratted, he'll be nothing but raw meat by the time I finish with him."

"Don't you think he knows that? He's a bright boy—or he can be." Maude glanced down the road. "That's probably him now."

Another older model car, this one a dusty beige, rolled to a stop next to Maude's blue one. A young guy about Jennie's age, maybe older, climbed out of the vehicle and headed straight toward her Mustang.

"Whoa! Great car." Frowning, he flipped his longish brown hair back. "I thought we were just doing junkers."

"We are." Jon retold his story about Jennie's car being the only one available.

"No kidding. Can we keep it?"

"No, we can't keep it." Maude sneered at him. "It's stolen. Sooner or later her parents are going to report her and the car missing."

"So maybe we could paint it or something."

"You knucklehead." Jon knocked the kid alongside the head.

Junior stumbled back, then caught himself. Jaw clenched, he gave Jon a murderous look. Jennie cringed. She felt sorry for the kid and hoped Jon wouldn't hit him again. She thought it odd that Jon would react so angrily to a suggestion he himself had made only hours before. Then, considering Maude's reaction, maybe not. Jennie had a feeling it was Maude, not Jon, who ran the show.

Jon raised his hands and shoved at Junior again. This time Junior went sprawling, landing in the gravel on his backside.

Maude stepped between them. "Stop it, both of you. I got enough to do without patching him up."

"I want an apology. Smart-aleck kid is always mouthing off about something."

Watching the anger flare between the three of them gave Jennie an idea: Junior might be her ticket out.

"S-sorry," Junior said at Maude's prompting. He scrambled to his feet and brushed off the back of his baggy pants. Like someone who'd been hit so many times he'd grown used to it, Junior recovered quickly. "So what are you going to do with it?"

The woman answered. "The two of you are going to hide the car and make sure no one finds it for another twenty years. If we're real lucky, they'll think she ran off the road somewhere up in the mountains and won't make any connection to the bank robberies or any of the vehicle thefts. Up until now no one's ever connected one of our cars with the robberies."

"Still don't know how that could have happened. The owner should have been at work all day."

"Things happen," Maude said. "But look on the bright side, you were able to get rid of the car and we're all here. Wonder who their suspect is."

"I don't know," Jon said, "but let's hope whatever rabbit trail they picked up will keep them busy for a while."

"What about the girl?" Junior picked a piece of gravel out of his hand.

Maude pulled a pack of cigarettes out of her pocket and tapped the end. Pulling one out, she lit it. "We'll have to kill her."

8

"Now, hold on, Maude." Jon glanced Jennie's way. "We agreed that we wouldn't—"

"That was before you saw fit to bring her here. We can't risk her identifying us."

"How's she gonna do that? Ain't none of us got a police record. Besides, with our makeup and wigs we look different with each job. I don't see no reason to shoot her. Figured we'd just leave her here. We'll be long gone before anybody finds her."

Jennie cheered the man on. *Listen to him, Maude.*

Maude screwed her face up as if it hurt her to think. "Maybe you're right. We didn't get into this business to hurt anybody."

Not hurt anybody? Jennie felt like throwing something and would have but thought better of it. No sense attracting attention to herself. Maybe if she pretended not to be a threat, they'd leave her alone. She didn't mind being left behind at the cabin. She was strong and had a good sense of direction. It might take her a couple of days, but she'd make it to the main road. From there it was only a matter of time before someone came along to help.

Junior ambled up to the porch and leveled his curious gaze on the shed, then sat down on the step. "So what does she look like?"

"Pretty." Jon gave him a sly grin. "Real pretty."

"Forget the girl." Maude cast both of them a disgusted

51

look. "The only one she's seen so far is Jon, and he was still in his disguise, right?"

"Yeah, sure," Jon lied. At least Jennie thought he must have. He looked the same now as when he'd hijacked her car.

"Good." Maude went on as though she hadn't noticed the slight pause. "She hasn't seen us, and there's no reason why she should have to."

"How we gonna accomplish that?" Jon asked. "I don't want to be putting on a wig and makeup every time we feed her and let her out to use the facilities."

"We won't have to. You two just stay out of sight and let me handle her." Maude stomped up the stairs. "And get rid of that blasted red car while I figure out a place to store the girl. We're probably okay for now, but I don't want to take the chance on having a search plane or chopper spotting it."

Jennie swallowed hard as she watched the three of them move out of her line of vision. Lowering herself into the chair, she closed her eyes. She'd much rather have had Jon or Junior in charge. Maude had about as much sympathy as a rabid bat.

Less, she decided when Maude yanked opened the door to the shed and ordered Jennie out. Jennie shielded her eyes from the sudden light. As her eyes adjusted, Jennie bit back a scream. Even knowing who Maude was hadn't prepared her for the woman's grotesquely distorted face. She'd put a black nylon stocking over her head. Maude loomed closer, looking like something out of a horror movie.

Jennie put on a mask of her own. She had to act scared and pretend she had no idea who this person was. *Act scared?* Who was she kidding? She was terrified. If Maude had any idea how much Jennie knew, she'd already be dead.

"Wh-who are you?" Jennie stammered.

"None of your business." Maude grabbed her arm and hauled Jennie to her feet. "Only thing you need to know is that if you try anything, I won't hesitate to put a bullet through your head."

Maude glanced around the shed. "What have you been doing in here?"

"N-nothing. I didn't want to sit on the floor so I took out a chair." Jennie held her breath as Maude examined the cluttered space. Jennie had plugged the knothole with a piece of brown paper bag so her captors wouldn't know she'd been watching them. To her, the plug stood out like tar on a white dog, but Maude didn't seem to notice. She propelled Jennie out onto the porch.

"What are you going to do with me?" Jennie gasped.

"You'll see soon enough. Get in the house."

Jennie stepped inside but got no farther than the entry. Maude opened the coat closet and shoved her in. "That ought to hold you."

Maude slammed the door against Jennie's backside. Jennie grabbed for the clothes rod to steady herself. Darkness assaulted her again.

Oh, God, what am I going to do now?

You're going to make it out of here, she reminded herself. *How?*

Jennie took several long, deep breaths to quell the panic bubbling up in her chest. *Calm down, McGrady. You've been in worse situations, and God has always helped you find a way out. He'll never leave you or forsake you.* It was an assurance she'd read many times in the Bible.

Jennie leaned against the wall, determined not to give up. *Think, McGrady, think. There is a way out. You may be locked in, but . . .*

Locked? No. She hadn't seen a lock of any kind on the closet door. Maude had simply closed it.

Jennie reached for the door handle. It turned. Her heart pounded as she eased the door open a crack. Maude was standing in the entry. Taking care not to make a sound, Jennie closed the door again. Her mind churned with possibilities for escape. All she had to do was wait until her captors were asleep.

"Help me move this sofa." Maude's scratchy voice tore apart Jennie's confidence.

"Where to?" Jon asked.

"I put her in the closet. Figure this thing will keep her there."

He grunted. "You're right about that. Feels like it's made out of bricks."

"It's one of those Hide-A-Beds."

The sleeper sofa scraped along the slate entry and thumped against the closet door. If it had taken two of them to move it, she wouldn't stand a chance of getting out.

Don't think that way, McGrady. You're strong. You've moved sofas before. When the time comes you'll push the door open. It'll work. It has to.

Would it? Jennie tried to hold on to the positive thought, but it slipped out of her grasp when she heard Maude telling Jon how they were going to have to take turns keeping watch to make sure Jennie didn't get away.

"What are we going to do with her tomorrow when we leave?" Jon asked. "She looks like a strong kid. She'll try to break out."

"Trust me, Jon. That girl isn't going anywhere."

"Yes, I am," Jennie muttered to herself, trying not to let Maude's comment get to her.

"What did you do with her car?" Maude must have moved away from the entry; Jennie could barely hear her.

"We took care of it. By the time we're done you won't even be able to see it from the ground. Drove it into a thicket of blackberry vines. Told Junior to put a camouflage tarp over it and cut down some fir branches."

"Good. Would have been better if we hadn't had to mess with it at all."

"I told you, I didn't have much choice."

"I know." Maude's voice softened. "You did what you had to do." She chuckled. "Main thing is we pulled it off. Only two more banks to go, and then we'll move on."

"Can't wait to get down to Mexico," Jon said. "We're gonna have us a great time. Maybe we could take a cruise, honey. You've always wanted to do that. Be like a second honeymoon."

"Hmm. Now, that sounds romantic. But what'll we do with Junior?"

"Take him along. We can afford to get him his own state-room."

"And then some," Maude agreed.

Jennie couldn't imagine anything romantic about going on a cruise with someone like Maude or Jon. She shuddered, then focused back to what they were saying. She had to remember every detail for the police. One way or another, Jennie wanted all three of them behind bars, and she'd do whatever it took to get them there.

The sound of sizzling meat made Jennie's stomach growl. The tantalizing scent wafted into the closet. Grilled steak or hamburgers, she guessed. She listened while they ate and cleaned up the dishes and talked about their next job. They'd hit Woodland and Longview the next day, then head for southern Oregon.

Jennie tried to ignore the hunger pangs, concentrating instead on devouring the information they were feeding her. They talked as though they'd forgotten she was there. Maybe they had.

Her back and hips ached from sitting on the hardwood floor. She'd been up and down a hundred times trying to find a comfortable position. Though she'd dragged a couple of jackets off the hangers, they did little to pad her bottom. She stood, massaging her sore muscles.

She hadn't eaten since breakfast. It had to be well past dinnertime.

They aren't going to feed you. By the time they leave you'll be too weak to hike out.

No, you won't, she argued against the pessimistic voice. *When they leave tomorrow you'll have several hours to yourself. You're strong. You've had survival skills training.*

Right, but how would she survive the night?

9

At the moment Jennie felt anything but strong. Her mouth was cotton dry. Her throat hurt. And she needed to go to the bathroom. She was cold. The temperature had dropped at least twenty degrees, and while her captors likely had the heat on, little of it reached her. The closet was on an outside wall.

Jennie shivered and rubbed at the goose bumps on her arms. Her jacket was still in her car. She felt around for one of the jackets she'd found hanging in the closet and slipped it on. It had a soft, cottony lining and smelled musty. She just hoped nothing creepy had taken up residence in it.

"Hey!" She banged on the door and yelled for them to let her out. "I need to go to the bathroom."

Maude let loose with a string of four-letter words. "Hold your horses. I'm coming. You should have shot her and left her in the woods with that old beater. S'pose you never even thought of that."

"We agreed there'd be no killing unless it was absolutely necessary. Far as I'm concerned, she don't pose a problem for us."

"Humph."

"Please," Jennie yelled again. "I'm not going to try to escape."

"The girl's trouble. I can feel it in my bones. Besides that, she looks familiar." Still muttering, Maude enlisted the help of Jon and Junior to move the heavy couch.

"Come on out," Maude said finally.

Jennie pushed on the door. It bumped against the back of the sofa, giving her just a little over a foot of space through which to squeeze. It was enough. The men were gone. Maude, wearing the nylon mask, had donned a heavy brown corduroy jacket. She waved her gun at Jennie and motioned her out the front door.

"Um . . . do you think I could have something to eat when we come back in?"

"Nothing left," Maude growled. "And don't be whining about it. If it was up to me, you'd be dead by now."

Jennie didn't doubt that one bit. She was an inconvenience, and Maude didn't like inconveniences. Jennie hurried outside. At least in the bathroom she could get water. People had been known to survive for days on water.

The porch light carved a dim path to the outhouse. Beyond the periphery, darkness reigned, offering yet another possibility of escape. Remembering the flashlight in the outhouse, Jennie drew in a long, shaky breath.

The flashlight, made of a sturdy black rubber-like material, had an easy nonslip grip. It had felt solid in her hand, like a club. Jennie walked in front of Maude and imagined herself raising the light and bringing it down on Maude's head, then running through the clearing and into the deep, dark woods. They'd never be able to catch her there. She'd run for an hour, then find a shelter of some kind and . . .

Her fantasies of escape ended briefly when they reached the outhouse. Jennie hurried inside, closed the door, and switched on the light. "This may take a while," Jennie told Maude.

Seconds later Jennie caught a whiff of cigarette smoke and heard the soft crunch of footsteps as Maude paced back and forth in front of the outhouse. Good. If she could pinpoint Maude's location she might be able to slip out and attack her from behind. Jennie turned the faucet on in a small stream so Maude wouldn't hear it. She let the water run cold, then bent her head to drink from her cupped hands. She savored the cool, fresh feel of it in her mouth and throat, taking in as much as she dared. She turned off the faucet and wiped her hands, then reached into the drawer to secure the flashlight—her weapon. Her stomach knotted with anticipation as she prepared herself for the next step.

Ear to the door, Jennie counted the steps. Seven to the right. Turn. Eight to the left. Eight right, then left. She envisioned Maude moving away from, then toward her. Jennie would have to make her move as Maude crossed in front of the door heading left. She'd turn the knob and raise the flashlight, then—

"What'd you do, fall asleep in there?" Maude barked. "Hurry up. It's freezing out here."

Jennie's heart slammed against her chest. The pattern had been broken. "I'm sorry. Shouldn't be much longer." She listened again, relieved when the pacing continued in much the same way.

When she thought Maude was passing the door, Jennie switched off the ceiling light and froze. Why hadn't she thought of it before? Surely Maude would notice she'd turned the light out.

Or would she? Beams from the yard light illuminated the small bathroom. Only one way to find out.

Jennie pressed down the handle and stepped outside. Maude had her back to Jennie. With a firm grip on the flashlight, she raised it high. Perfect. Jennie flung herself forward and slammed her weapon against what should have been the base of Maude's skull. Instead, Jennie's blow grazed Maude's shoulder.

"What in the—" Maude spun around and shoved her fist into Jennie's midsection.

Jennie doubled over and stumbled back, gasping for breath.

"Why, you little . . ." Maude closed in, sending Jennie to her knees with a blow to the back of her neck. Then Maude dove on top of her. "Jon, get out here!"

Jennie struggled against her, trying to push her off.

"I ought to kill you right here and now."

Jennie felt the cool steel of the gun barrel against her temple. She closed her eyes and waited for the explosion that would end her life. Her breaths came in snatches. Shallow. Pained. Attempts at prayer fell into two words. *God, please.*

10

Stupid, stupid, stupid. Jennie leaned back against the closet wall. She'd miscalculated her own strength and especially Maude's—big time. Maude was smaller than Jennie, more wiry, but much stronger. Jennie had been so sure of herself. Maybe Maude had heard the door or seen the light go off. Maybe she was waiting, knowing Jennie would try something. Maude would have done something like that just so she could beat her up.

You should have just run away. Or waited until they were gone.

Get a grip, McGrady, part of her insisted. *You did what you had to do. You'd do it again if you got the chance.*

What does is matter? You can't go back. It's too late to think about what you should or shouldn't have done. Jennie grimaced. *Chances are you'll never get another chance.* They'd tied her up with a rough nylon cord, hands behind her back, ankles secured. The only thing she'd managed to do so far was to slip her body through the loop her arms made and bring her hands to the front. Her mouth and wrists were already worn raw from her attempts to loosen the bonds with her teeth.

She licked her dry, bleeding lips where the stiff and unyielding rope fibers had cut into her tender skin. It seemed like hours since she'd been to the outhouse. Tears gathered in her eyes. And this time she didn't try to stop them. It was the first time she'd cried since they'd picked her up off the ground and locked her back in the closet.

Even though they'd tied her up, Maude had insisted that Junior sleep on the couch. Jennie hadn't even tried to open the door. The sofa was still shoved up against it.

After a while she gave up on crying. It wasn't doing any good, and all she'd managed to get out of it was a wet face, a stuffy nose, and salt in her wounds. Jennie sniffled, then freed the bottom of her T-shirt from her jeans and used it to wipe off her face.

"It's not the end of the world, Jennie," she imagined her mother saying. Maybe it wasn't the end of the world yet, but Jennie suspected it was only a matter of time.

Jennie shifted around and, using a jacket as a pillow, curled up on her side. Maybe if she could sleep, the time would go faster. She'd just lowered her head when she heard a scraping sound. Someone was moving the couch. Had Maude decided to get rid of her after all?

The closet door opened. Muted moonlight coming in through the windows eased away the darkness. Junior's shadowy bulk filled the opening. Jennie, more curious than frightened, scooted against the back wall. "What do you want?"

"Shh." He hunkered down in front of her. "I brought you some food and water," he whispered. "It isn't much— just a sandwich I made from the leftover meat."

Leftover? Maude had told her there was nothing left. "Thank you." Jennie grabbed for the sandwich and began stuffing it into her mouth. Her lips burned, but she ignored the pain.

"I was going to make myself a snack and remembered . . . my aunt should have fed you."

Jennie took another bite and nodded in agreement. After inhaling half the sandwich, Jennie reached for the water he'd set on the floor beside her. "I really appreciate this, Junior."

"Name's not Junior. It's Zack. My aunt and uncle call me that because they know I hate it."

"Mmm." Jennie met his gaze and said, "Why are you staying with them?"

He looked away. "I wish I didn't have to. But if I didn't live with them, I'd have to go to foster care. They're the only family I have. My parents died when I was ten, and Aunt Maude and Uncle Jon took me in. Jon is my father's brother. It's not so bad now."

"Foster care? But aren't you old enough to live on your own?" Looking at him close up, she figured he had to be at least eighteen.

His lips curled in a crooked smile. "I just turned fourteen in August."

"Could have fooled me."

"Yeah. I fool a lot of people."

"I don't get it. You're only fourteen and they've got you driving and robbing banks?"

He sucked in a sharp breath and backed away as if she'd slapped him. "It's better than . . . Listen, I . . ." He took a blanket off the couch and handed it to her. "You might need this."

"Thanks, Zack. You seem like a nice guy." Jennie caught his arm. "Listen, I could help you get away from them."

He gave her a wry smile. "I don't think so. Doesn't look like you're in much of a position to help anybody."

"That could change if you'd help me escape. We could take my car and get away tonight—right now."

Zack shook his head. "Jon has the keys and your car is . . ." He stood. "I can't do that."

"But—"

He scooped up the napkin and glass. "No."

Zack closed the door, ending their discussion. Jennie stared into the darkness for several long moments, hoping he'd change his mind. Praying he'd come back. When he didn't, she wrapped the blanket around her and tried to make sense of what had just happened.

Zack was an unwilling participant in all this. A minor. He had given her food, but more importantly he'd given a generous serving of hope. He'd said no to helping her get away, but that didn't mean she couldn't eventually change his mind.

Jennie spent the rest of the night half sleeping, half awake, thinking about Zack and wondering what it would take to convince him to help her. She thought about Nick and wondered how he was doing on his sleepover. Was he scared? She hoped not. She thought about Jeremiah's invitation to stay at the farm and wished more than anything she'd accepted. She thought about Lisa and Scott and Gavin and wondered how long it had taken them to report her missing.

What were her parents doing? Jennie knew they wouldn't be sleeping either. Had they called Gram and J.B.? Were they all congregated at the McGrady house, talking to police, heading up a search? Last summer, when Nick had been missing, the house became a command center. They'd put out missing-child posters and searched the entire neighborhood. The police had been quick to act then. A missing child.

But Jennie wasn't a child. The police might not even be looking for her. Maybe they'd think she ran away. The family would know better, wouldn't they? Of course. Dad would talk to them. They were probably out there searching for her right now. *Don't give up. I love you. I'm here. I'm alive. I miss you.*

They'll never find you. They'll be looking for your car, and it's hidden, an unbidden voice countered.

Hot tears burned her cheeks again. *Only a miracle can save you now.*

Jennie closed her eyes again and prayed, trying to place her fate in God's hands. Maybe she couldn't escape on her own, but she had to keep believing—though that was getting harder all the time.

11

Morning brought smells and sounds of breakfast—bacon, eggs, and toast. Hunger pangs urged Jennie into a foggy wakefulness. Maude wouldn't be feeding her, and she doubted Zack would be able to slip her anything this morning unless they left him alone.

"Wonder how our prisoner slept last night," Jon said.

"Don't know and don't plan to ask." Maude coughed. "She can rot in there for all I care."

Jon laughed. "You should've known better than to turn your back on her. Gotta give her credit, though. She's a scrappy kid."

"That's not exactly the word I'd use. The kid is a major pain. I'll be glad when we're rid of her."

"Junior." Jon's voice again. "You and me'll have to go car shopping up in Longview before we hit the bank up there. Want you to drive the new car to the Triangle Mall and wait for me there. We'll head on down to Woodland and pick Maude up at the Dairy Queen. It's just off the freeway. Then we'll take the back roads and meet back here. Any preference on the car, Maude?"

"Just make sure it'll get us to eastern Oregon."

"Thought I'd spend a little more. Get something newer."

"Not too much. We gotta make this money last us awhile. And for pity's sake get something besides beige or gray. Maybe something blue—not too bright, though."

"You want me to feed Jennie and walk her to the out-house?" Zack asked.

"Jennie? Since when did you start calling her that?" Maude's tone was whip sharp and mean. "You fed her last night, didn't you? I noticed that extra hamburger was gone."

"I got hungry during the night and fixed myself a sand-wich," Zack answered. "And why shouldn't I call her Jen-nie? That's her name, ain't it?"

"Don't you be talking back to your auntie, boy," Jon threatened. "Not unless you want to see the back of my hand."

Jennie winced as a chair scraped back and crashed to the floor.

"I wasn't talking back. Just think we should treat her like a human being. Even a dog gets table scraps."

"Better a dog than her," Maude responded.

No one spoke for a time. The chair got righted, and Jen-nie could hear the clink of utensils on plates. Then water running. She could only hope Jon's threats and Maude's surliness worked to her advantage. If they were mean enough to Zack, maybe she'd be able to convince him to escape and take her with him.

"Here," Maude said. "Give her this and take her to the outhouse. Just make sure she don't get away."

The sofa scraped across the floor again, and the door opened. This time it was Jon who handed her the food. He hadn't bothered to disguise himself. But then, why should he? She'd already seen him when he abducted her. Only Maude didn't know that.

"What'd you do to your mouth?" He actually looked like he cared.

"I was hungry. Tried to eat the rope."

Jon laughed like Jennie had told the biggest joke he'd ever heard. "Left a bad taste in your mouth, did it?"

The corner of Jennie's mouth twitched. "Yeah. You might say that."

He hitched a hip on the back of the couch and watched

her choke down the cold scrambled eggs and toast. She ate it all without complaining. After all, it was fuel for her journey home. When she finished he walked her to the outhouse. Jennie had to wait outside until Maude finished getting ready. Maude came out wearing a red wig. She'd changed her skin tone, probably by using one of those tanning lotions. And she wore an excess of makeup that made her appear almost clownlike.

"What do you think, Jon?" She batted her eyes at him.

"Good one. Better go see how Junior's coming with his." Jon chuckled. "He was complaining about having to dress up like a girl."

"Too bad you can't go with us, Jennie," Maude said in a heavy southern accent. "I bet you'd get a kick out of seein' our performance. We're good, baby, real good."

"I'm sure you are," Jennie said sarcastically. "But sooner or later the police will catch up with you. They always do."

"Not always." Maude sent Jennie a withering look and headed toward the house.

Jennie used the facilities, then took a few minutes to wash her face and hands. Everything took about twice as long as it would have had she not had the rope around her wrists, but at least she could still maneuver somewhat.

She looked as if she'd been run through a meat grinder. She had two black eyes and bruises on over half her face from her encounter with Maude. Her lips were puffy and scabbed with dried blood. She wet down a washcloth and pressed it against her face. After soaking her lips for a minute, she wished she could get to her backpack to retrieve her Chap Stick. Maybe . . . Jennie checked the medicine cabinet and drawer where she'd seen the first-aid supplies. In one of the drawers she found a small jar of Vaseline and in another a tube of antibiotic ointment. She slipped both into her pocket. Her gaze fell to the small plastic garbage container and the disposable razor that had been discarded. She scooped that up as well.

Jon was waiting when she came out. She didn't even

think about getting away this time. She had to save her energy. Sooner or later she'd make her move. She had a razor blade. Now at least she could get rid of the ropes.

When her captors left, Jennie used the razor to cut through the stubborn knots. After applying the antibiotic lotion to the sores on her face and wrists, Jennie put the Vaseline on her lips. Then she spent all of five minutes trying to get out of the closet. As she'd suspected, they'd shoved something else in front of the door. Her only other chance was to remove the hinges. Unfortunately, they were on the outside.

Face it, McGrady. There's nothing to do now but wait.

———

The sounds of cars crunching through gravel brought her up and to her knees. They'd come back. Within minutes the entire gang was at the table eating lunch and talking about how they'd outsmarted the cops once again. They'd collected over five hundred thousand dollars in two days. Maude and Jon bragged about how they had the cops running in circles.

"We're home free," Jon said.

"Don't be so sure." Maude sounded tired. "I won't be able to rest until we're in Mexico. I've been thinking maybe we ought to head out today."

"Now, honey, there's no hurry. We'll rest here and have a nice barbecue. Maybe we can take the canoe out on the river. Might as well enjoy the place while we can."

"Didn't you hear what that reporter said on the radio? The girl's father is a cop, for crying out loud."

Jennie's heart thumped hard against her chest. The authorities were looking for her. She knew they would be, but it helped to hear the words spoken aloud.

"Maude, take it easy. There's no connection between her and us. They think her car went off the road somewhere between Battle Ground and that campground where I picked her up, just like we thought they would."

Maude heaved a loud sigh. "I suppose you're right.

We'll leave first thing in the morning, though. I want everything packed up tonight."

"That's my girl. What route do you want to take?"

Jennie caught the last sentence and listened more carefully. She'd need all the information she could get for when she talked to the authorities.

"We'll take the back roads around Mount Adams and come out by Carson. I think we ought to stay on the Washington side of the gorge till we get to Umatilla and cross over to Oregon there."

"Might be best to hide out in eastern Oregon for a few days," Maude added. "Always wanted to see the Wallowa Mountains."

"Sounds good. What do you say we hit a couple banks in Bend and Redmond on the way?" Jon suggested.

"I don't know. We were pushing our luck doing the ones we did today."

They were talking so freely now, Jennie wondered if they'd forgotten about her.

That's not the case and you know it.

They weren't going to be happy when they learned she'd untied the ropes. Again she wished she had her grandmother's martial arts training—or any kind of training. She could wipe them all out. But as Mom would say, *"If wishes were fishes . . ."*

"Well, I'll be." Jennie heard a newspaper rustling. Maude made another crude remark. "You sure know how to pick 'em, Jon. Take a look at this."

"You want me to make a sandwich for Jennie?" Zack asked.

"Sure, why not," Maude said. "In fact, bring her out to the table."

Something about Maude's generosity sent a chill through Jennie. *They know your dad's a cop. Do you really think they're going to let you live?* She shoved the ominous feeling aside and waited for the door to open.

Zack sent her a warning look as he opened the door. He apparently didn't want her telling his aunt and uncle about their talk the night before. He needn't have worried. Jennie had no intention of telling them anything.

His gaze dropped to her wrists and feet. "How did you. . . ?" He stopped and glanced toward Maude and Jon. "She's got herself untied."

"Don't worry about it." Maude looked up from the newspaper she had spread out on the table. "She ain't goin' nowhere."

Fear rumbled in the pit of Jennie's stomach, sending tremors through her whole body.

"There's sandwich makings on the counter. Help yourself." Maude snagged a gun from beside the sink and set it on the table beside her plate.

"Thanks." Jennie swallowed hard, trying not to think about what the attitude change meant. She tried not to think about the fact that they now knew she was a cop's daughter, Or that they no longer minded her seeing them without their disguises. Or that Maude seemed very interested in something she was reading in the paper. Instead, she focused on making her tuna sandwich.

Jennie sliced a dill pickle and placed the pieces over the tuna salad, then topped it with lettuce and another slice of bread. After grabbing a few baby carrots and some tortilla chips, she sat in the chair next to Zack.

"Want some milk?" Maude asked. Without waiting for an answer, she asked Zack to get a glass.

He set the glass in front of Jennie and filled it, his gaze briefly meeting hers, then guiltily flitting away. She looked at the other two, but only one made eye contact. Maude.

"Jon and I were talking about you on the way back," she said. "We been trying to figure out what to do with you. He still thinks we should leave you here. I disagree."

Jennie took a bite of sandwich, pretending not to be concerned. It tasted like sawdust. She took a drink of milk to wash it down.

"We thought about taking you with us, but . . ." Maude glanced at Zack and grimaced. "We got enough trouble with Junior here. Besides, you wouldn't be happy traveling with us. Oh, we could use you as a hostage if we needed one, but I don't expect we will."

Jennie looked at the sandwich and set it down. Dread had eaten away any trace of hunger she might have had. Jennie knew exactly where Maude was going. The paper showed pictures of her and her family.

"The cops think you were out looking for us." Maude folded up the paper and set it aside.

"What are you talking about?" Zack asked.

Maude ignored him. "Is that true, Jennie?"

"No. I . . . I was meeting my friends at the trailhead."

"Why would you think that?" Zack persisted.

"Remember when I said I'd seen her before? Well, I was right. Couldn't place her until I read about her in the paper. She's the kid who came into the Lake Oswego bank while we were robbing it."

Maude wiped her mouth with the napkin and smiled. "Much as it hurts us to do it, we just plain have to kill you."

12

"There, now," Maude soothed. "I've gone and spoiled your appetite."

Jennie wasn't sure how she managed to speak. All she knew was that she couldn't give up. It just wasn't an option—not for a McGrady. Meeting Maude's stony gaze, Jennie took another drink of milk. "Not at all. I've known from the beginning you weren't going to let me go."

Maude cocked an eyebrow. "Aren't you smart! Considering we didn't know ourselves."

"You knew."

"Maybe I did."

"The point is," Jennie went on, "I'm not the least bit worried." Okay, so maybe she was a little worried. But she felt certain her faith would sustain her. She knew in her heart God would never abandon her.

That doesn't mean He's going to let you live. People with faith die all the time. Jennie pushed the unwanted thoughts out of her mind.

Maude sneered at her. "Maybe you didn't hear me right."

With more bravado than she felt, Jennie said, "You can kill me, but I won't die."

"Oh, don't worry, we'll make sure you're dead."

Jennie's throat went dry. She took another sip of milk. "Maybe physically I will, but I'll go to heaven and—"

"Did you hear that, Jon? She's going to heaven. What'll you do then? Haunt us?"

"I won't need to. God will. He'll dig himself into your conscience and make you pay for what you're doing." That assurance gave her renewed strength. "The police are going to track you down. You think you're so smart with all these disguises and switching cars. Well, you're not going to get away with it. The police have dozens of clues. A fingerprint, a hair . . ."

"We don't leave clues." Maude looked a little less sure of herself.

"Yes, you do. All criminals do. Especially amateurs like you."

Maude's fake tan deepened and her jaw clenched. She pushed her chair back and picked up the gun.

Jennie sucked in a deep breath and sat up straighter. If she had to die, she'd do it with dignity. Maude was at her side in a second, her left hand gripping Jennie's hair, forcing her to her feet.

"Not in the cabin, Maude." Jon laid a warning hand on his wife's arm. "We don't want anyone to find her, remember? Shoot her here and there'll be blood all over the place."

"Then I'll take her out in the woods and shoot her now."

"Not until we're ready to leave. I told you I'd take care of it in the morning."

"What's the difference? Never mind." Maude shoved Jennie onto the chair and sat back down. "You're right. Police are probably searching the entire mountain right now looking for that car. Gunshots would just draw their attention."

"I'll take care of her tomorrow morning just before we leave. That way if anybody does hear the shots, we'll be long gone before they can figure out where they came from."

Jennie blinked back tears and stole a glance at Zack, trying to measure whether she'd find an ally in him. The muscle in Zack's jaw twitched. His Adam's apple bobbed up and down.

Maude must have noticed his obvious discomfort. "You okay with that, Junior?"

"Why are you asking me? You and Uncle Jon do whatever you want. Doesn't matter what I think."

"You're not going soft on us, are you?"

" 'Course not." He scraped back his chair and took his plate and glass to the sink, washed them off, and set them on the drying rack.

But he *was* going soft. Jennie could sense it. He didn't want them to kill her. He didn't want to be there, period.

God, she offered up another prayer, *please let me convince Zack to help me get away. Please.*

Surprisingly, Maude allowed Jennie to finish her lunch. She'd lost her appetite after the first bite but forced the rest of the sandwich, milk, and chips down, fiercely clinging to the hope that God would send a miracle her way.

While Jennie ate, Jon enlisted Zack's help in bringing in their loot from the trunk of their new car, a silvery-blue Bonneville. They set four black garbage bags in the entry and went out again, this time to the shop.

Jon and Zack carried in a dozen more bags. Just before Maude ushered Jennie back to the closet, Jon emptied one of the bags on the table. Bills tumbled out in a mass array of green—packs of tens, twenties, fifties, and hundred-dollar bills covered the table and slipped onto the floor. Jennie couldn't remember seeing that much money in her life.

"Bet you're itching to get your hands on some of that, huh?" Maude's eyes glinted with greed.

"No, actually. I wouldn't take it if you paid me. It's dirty."

"Well, Miss High and Mighty. Maybe it's time you got dirtied up a mite." Maude scooped up a handful and rubbed it on Jennie's face, then let it drift to the floor.

Jennie tried to pull away. Maude held her arm for a moment, then let go. Jennie stumbled and fell. For the first time since she'd been taken captive, Jennie couldn't wait to get into the closet so she wouldn't have to look at them.

They didn't give her dinner that night. Zack didn't ask, and neither Jon nor Maude mentioned her. At least they hadn't tied her up this time. For a while Jennie wondered if they were even going to let her out to go to the bathroom. It was after ten when Maude finally came to take her outside. This time she smoked her cigarette but obviously had no intention of letting down her guard.

Jennie hurried through her routine, drinking as much as she could hold and washing up. She used some of the toothpaste she'd found earlier, rubbing it on her teeth with her finger, then rinsing her mouth. Funny how you never thought twice about things like toothbrushes until you no longer had them. She was almost desperate enough to use one of the brushes in the holder—almost. The thought of putting one of their brushes in her mouth made her gag. She took as long as she dared, then trudged back to the house.

Zack slept on the couch again and surprised Jennie by bringing her a snack of cold chicken and a glass of water around midnight.

"Thanks," Jennie whispered. "I didn't think you'd bother, seeing as they're going to—" Her throat closed up.

"I'm sorry about that. Wish there was something I could do."

"There is, Zack. You can let me go. Right now."

"I told you before, I can't do that. You have no idea what they'd do to me. I'm one of them, and nothing you or I do is going to change that."

"You can get help. Foster care isn't so bad."

"No way. I'm a criminal. If I got caught I'd spend the rest of my life in jail."

"No, you wouldn't. You're a minor. I can help you. My dad's a cop, remember? If you help me, he'll make sure you don't even have to do time. Please. You can't keep going like this. Sooner or later your aunt and uncle will get caught and you'll go down with them."

"It's no use, Jennie. Besides, things aren't so bad for me now, especially when they're bringing in money. Jon doesn't beat me up much anymore. As long as I go along with them I'm okay."

It's not okay. Far from it. Jennie wrapped the chicken bone in the napkin and handed it to him. "If you let them kill me, you'll be an accomplice to murder."

"There's nothing I can do."

"Fine." Jennie stepped out of the closet. "I'm going without you."

He looked surprised. "Now?"

She brushed past him. For a brief moment Jennie actually thought he was going to let her go.

"No." He grabbed for her.

She yanked her arm out of his grasp. "How are you going to stop me?"

His arm shot out and snagged her waist, bringing her up against him. He twisted her right arm behind her, pressing it up until she gasped in pain.

"Let me go." Jennie struggled to get away.

He tightened his hold.

"Zack, please. You're not like them." Jennie felt his grip loosen. She spun around and yanked her arm free. She ran for the door and pulled it open.

Zack reached around her and slammed it hard, shaking the entire house. "Now you've done it!"

"What's going on down there?" Jon yelled.

"Nothing," Zack called toward the stairs. "I was just coming in from the outhouse. The wind caught the door."

Jon mumbled something unintelligible, then quieted down.

"I . . . I don't want to hurt you, Jennie, but I'm more scared of him than I am of you."

"I'm sorry for you, Zack." He was strong and big for his age. She might be able to outrun him. But any further attempt to escape would bring Jon and Maude running. And Zack would bear the brunt of their anger. She shouldn't care, but she did.

She turned around and headed back to the closet. Folding her arms, she lowered herself to the floor. "Deep down you're as bad as they are."

"I'm not. It's just . . ."

"Then you're a coward."

"M-maybe I am."

"Here." She shoved the water at him and closed the door.

Jennie wondered if her confrontation had any effect on him at all. Maybe he'd think about what she'd said and in the end . . .

Who are you kidding, McGrady. The kid's scared to death of his aunt and uncle.

He's a coward. A stinking, rotten . . .

He's a kid, a more sympathetic side of her reminded. *He's only fourteen.*

Yeah, but he could have helped. If it were me I'd help him.

He's been abused. You have no idea what he's been through.

"Maybe not," Jennie murmured aloud, but he could have changed things. Jennie had a hard time understanding why people made the choices they did. Zack didn't have to stay in an abusive situation. She remembered something her mother had said about how frightening things can look to an abuse victim. *"The situation they are in might be bad, but it's what they are used to. Sometimes it's easier to live in pain than to face the uncertainty of change."* Jennie wished she could convince him that he didn't have to stay. Yet she supposed in a way he did. She wondered how many beatings it had taken to turn him into such a pathetic wimp.

Jennie closed her eyes and said a prayer for Zack. He was missing a chance to be free. Tears gathered in her eyes as she thought about the childhood he'd lost and the pain he'd suffered. She cried for herself as well. Time was running out. Unless something happened soon, she'd never see her family again. Never read bedtime stories to Nick or pet Bernie's silky hair. She'd never see the baby her mother carried in her womb. She'd never be able to talk shop with Dad, Gram, or J.B. She'd always loved hearing about this case or that. Already she missed Lisa and her bubbly outlook on life. And Scott and Ryan.

Jennie imagined the grief she'd leave behind. Would there be a lot of people at her funeral? There would be no casket. Jennie doubted anyone would find her remains. She shuddered and dragged her thoughts away from the gruesome image.

Jennie spent the rest of the night thinking and dreaming about people she knew and saying good-bye to them. More than anything she wanted to keep her mind on escaping, but for some reason everyone she knew drifted in and out of her thoughts as the funeral of her dreams dragged on through the night.

———

Morning brought food smells and sounds of clinking dishes and silverware. Jennie reluctantly came awake. Thoughts of death had eventually brought a certain peace. Safely tucked away in a godly realm, she felt no pain, no fear, and no impending doom. Now, with the departure of her captors minutes away, the reality of her situation consumed her like a tidal wave, crashing, churning, offering no means of escape.

Her insides were a twisted mass of questions. Had the dream been a premonition of things to come? Should she stop thinking of getting away and let the inevitable happen?

Are you sure it is inevitable?

Maybe.

You can't give up. Her thoughts warred with one another again and again. In the end she knew that until she drew her last breath, she'd keep trying to escape. She'd fight to stay alive.

Jennie hadn't heard much talk so far. Mostly thumping noises and the sound of doors opening and closing. Then came some prodding on Maude's part to hurry the guys along. They were packing. Clearing out. The strong smell of Pine-Sol assaulted her nostrils.

"Please let them forget about me." Even as the whispered prayer left her lips, Jennie knew they wouldn't. She switched her pleas to finding a way out.

"All right," Maude said, "looks like we're all set. The Graham family won't know we were ever here. We've got one more chore and we're off. Jon, you ready?"

"Ready as I'll ever be."

"Look, if you can't do this, just give me the gun."

"I told you I'd take care of it," he grumped. "I'm the one who brought her here. Should be me who gets rid of her."

"Junior," Maude ordered, "come help me move this sofa back where it belongs."

Jennie's heart skittered to a stop. *This must be what it feels like to be on death row waiting for the executioner to open the cell and—*

The sofa screeched across the floor.

Jon opened the door. "It's time, little lady. You and I are going for a little walk."

13

Jennie couldn't talk. Her mouth had gone dry as an old desert bone. She wiped her palms on her jeans. Her legs had turned to mush, and she could barely put one foot in front of the other.

She could see Maude through the living room window, making the trek to the outhouse. Zack stood near the couch looking as if he were going to a funeral. Her gaze caught and held Zack's for one long moment as she silently pleaded with him to stop them.

He turned away. "I think I'll have one last look around," he told his uncle just before hurrying toward the house.

"Let's go." Jon prodded her in the side with the gun. "No sense prolonging things. Makes it harder on both of us."

Both of us? Jennie almost laughed at the irony of his comment. In a way he was right. In the long run killing her would be a lot harder on him than dying would be for her. She'd be gone, and he'd have to live with the memory of murdering a sixteen-year-old girl for the rest of his miserable life.

They walked along a short trail to the river, then went upstream about twenty feet to where the river widened. Someone had built a dock there. Jennie wondered if Jon was going to shoot her there by the river. She hoped he'd try it. She'd dive in before he could get a shot off, then swim to the other side.

But Jon steered her away from the water and into the thick forest that lined the river.

"How far are you taking me?" Jennie asked.

"Just far enough from the cabin so nobody's gonna find you. No need to go too far. Figure the owners probably won't be coming out into these woods any time soon. In a few days the animals will have dragged your carcass off to who knows where."

Jennie swallowed back the bile rising to her throat. She spent the next few minutes reminding herself that it didn't really matter what happened to her body. She'd still be alive and hanging out in heaven with God and the angels. *Lord, please. If you're going to give me a chance to escape, it has to be now.*

Run, an inner voice urged. *He'll kill you for sure if you don't.*

Jennie bolted. A gunshot ripped through the morning, exploding in her ears. A bullet sliced into a tree trunk near her head. She ducked, without breaking stride, weaving between the trees. Another shot.

The impact of bullet against bone brought her to her knees. Gritting her teeth, she struggled to get up. *Keep going. Run.*

Too late.

Jon slammed a fist into her side, forcing her onto her back. His furious gaze bore into hers. Searing pain ripped through her thigh. She grasped at the wound, trying to back away.

He aimed the gun at her heart. His lips curved in a demented smile. "I didn't want to kill you, girl. Tried to talk Maude into just leaving you at the cabin. But now . . ."

Jennie closed her eyes as he pulled the trigger.

Click.

Her breath gushed out in a half cry, half scream.

Click.

The gun had jammed, or he'd run out of bullets.

Jon swore and threw the gun aside. His fists clenched, he started toward her.

Clutching her leg, Jennie rolled over and tried to stand.

"Oh no, you don't." Jon hauled her to her feet and drew back his fist.

Jennie lifted her arms to protect her face. "Please, don't . . . I won't tell anyone I—"

She never got a chance to finish. One fist hit her raised arm. He rammed the other against her exposed jaw.

A scream caught in her throat. Jennie tripped on a root and staggered backward. Her arms flailed as she tried to break her fall. The back of her skull connected with something hard and unyielding. White light exploded through her head.

In the distance she heard a woman's voice. "Jon? What in tarnation is taking you so long? Let's go!"

"Coming," he yelled back. Leaves crunched under heavy footsteps. "Idiot girl," he mumbled. "I was only going to wound you and let you go. Now you've gone and killed yourself."

The footsteps faded into oblivion. A blessed darkness covered Jennie like a blanket. She felt herself being lifted up higher and higher. Looking down from her lofty perch, she could see a dark-haired girl with a bruised and swollen face lying on the ground. A tree stump pillowed her head. Blood seeped into her jeans at the thigh, turning the denim a deep burgundy. She lay at an odd angle, with fir and cedar towering around her like sentinels keeping watch.

In an instant the image was gone. Jennie felt a moment of excruciating pain at the back of her head. Then nothing.

14

Somewhere beyond the throbbing pain in her head, Jennie heard a mournful scream. A numblike state enveloped her. Was she dreaming? No, there were no images, only sounds—rustling leaves, chirping birds, the musty smell of earth and woods.

She heard the shrill cry again. A cougar?

Jennie's eyes flew open. The hairs on her neck and arms stiffened in alarm. Trees towered overhead. She tried sitting. The action sent a shooting pain through her head and thigh. She lay back down on her side, drawing in deep breaths. When the pain subsided, she gingerly touched the wide oval patch of dried blood on her jeans. The denim had a rip in it.

Why am I here—alone in the woods? She frowned, unable to remember.

What happened to my leg?

The cougar screeched again, a long, plaintive cry that seemed to go on forever. On the tail of the cougar's scream came the *yip-yip-yowl* of a coyote. Jennie caught a movement off to her right. At first she saw nothing but dappled sunlight filtering through the trees. Her eyes finally focused on a skinny gray-brown dog that stood in the shadow of a moss-covered log not more than thirty feet away.

No, not a dog. A coyote. Fear washed over her again and left her gasping for air. Her sharp cry sent the animal scampering away.

Jennie groaned. Another wave of pain shot through her.

She brought her hands to her head and rolled onto her back. She had no idea how she'd ended up in the woods or how she'd been hurt. But she did know one thing: She had to find shelter before nightfall. The dried blood on her pants would draw back the coyote and who knew what else. Cougars? Bears?

"God," she cried into the heavens. "Oh, God, what's happened to me. Where am I?"

Her raspy voice echoed in the stillness. There were no eerie sounds now. Only the light rustling of a wind stirring dry leaves on the forest floor. And something else. Water. A river or stream rushing over rocks.

Need to get to the water. Thirsty. So thirsty. Jennie licked her dry lips.

She tried again to move, but the pain came back, worse than before.

Don't move. You might have broken something. Jennie didn't know where the thought had come from. Only that it made sense.

But how could she stay?

Maybe if she rested for a few minutes the pain would eventually lessen and she'd try again.

Sometime later Jennie lifted her gaze to the sky, trying to get her bearings. The sun peeked through the forest with gentle fingers, turning the fallen leaves of a vine maple to burnished gold. She couldn't tell if it was coming up or going down. Going down, she guessed. Had to be, otherwise she'd be colder. Pink linings on the scattered clouds overhead suggested the sun had already begun its descent. She heard rustling in a nearby bush and heard a low, guttural growl.

A primal sense of urgency propelled her forward.

Again a searing pain knifed into the back of her skull, bringing with it a shock of light, then nothing.

A whining sound and a brush of moisture on her cheek

dragged Jennie into wakefulness.

Jennie brushed at her face. Her hand came in contact with something soft and furry. She smiled as the image of a dog with brown-and-white fur and large blue eyes filled her head.

A coyote let loose with a mournful cry. Jennie's heart leaped to her throat. He was back. Afraid to move, Jennie pressed her lips together, praying it wouldn't attack. Was it only one? What if there was a pack of them, circling, coming in for the kill?

The whining resumed. It didn't sound like a coyote. And as far as she knew, coyotes didn't lick their prey to death.

Jennie held her breath and opened her eyes. Her fears tumbled out in a sob. A dog. A big, friendly dog. Tears gathered in her eyes. The animal nudged her with its nose. The fast-fading light shone in his eyes. He pulled back as she reached out to pet him. In a moment he was back in her face, licking and whining. She stroked his silky hair. "Hey," she croaked. "Where did you come from?"

The dog ran several feet away from her, barked, then came back. He gave her a couple more licks, then loped into the woods, barking.

"Thank you, God," she whispered. *If there's a dog, there must be people.* Jennie lowered her arm. It hurt. Everything hurt. She remembered waking up and not being able to move. Her head still felt like it had been rammed with a tree trunk. Above her, trees as tall as mountains reached into the dusky blue sky.

"Lucy!" someone called. "Where are you?"

Jennie turned her head toward the voice and tried to sit up. That was a mistake. Another sharp pain ripped through her head and shoulders. "Help. Help me," she groaned in a voice barely audible to her own ears before lowering herself back to the ground.

"What was that?" one of the voices, a girl, asked.

"What?" another girl responded.

"That sound."

Jennie tried calling again, but her mouth was so dry she couldn't come up with much more than a hoarse whisper.

"I don't hear anything except Lucy. Take it easy, girl. What's out there, huh? Come on, Luce. Come back to the cabin. It's not safe out here."

"Lucy!" the voice rose in annoyance. "Come back here and quit fooling around."

"Hey, look, Brandy, she's trying to get us to follow her. See how she runs to us and then back into the woods? Let's go see what she's found."

"Don't, Corisa. It's probably a dead rabbit or something totally freaky. Dad said to stay close to the cabin."

"I know, but . . ."

The dog returned to Jennie's side, then ran off in the direction he'd come. He barked and growled, repeating the pattern several times.

"Help!" Jennie tried calling again. Rays of fading light broke free of the clouds and eased between the trees.

"Listen. I did hear something."

"All right. We'll follow her, but stay close to me. Here, give me the flashlight."

"No. I'll hold it."

"Then get in front of me."

"I'm too scared. Can't we just walk next to each other?"

Lucy barked again, racing toward Jennie. She licked her face again as if to say, "I've got it covered," then ran back to the girls. The light was stronger now. Jennie called out again.

"There. Someone is calling for help. I told you."

Jennie covered her eyes as the flashlight beam found her.

"Corisa, look."

Lucy nuzzled Jennie again.

"Good girl, Lucy." Two girls about Jennie's age hunkered down on either side of her. "Don't be scared," the smallest of the two said to Jennie. "I'm Brandy Graham, and this is my sister, Corisa. How did you get here?"

"Where did you come from?" Corisa asked.

"Are you hurt bad?"

Questions tumbled from their mouths, but Jennie could only groan in response.

"Looks like someone beat her up," Corisa said.

"And left her alone. Oh man, that is so scary. What if he's still around?"

"He isn't. I don't think anyone is or Lucy would be having a fit."

"Right."

Corisa, apparently the oldest, turned to Jennie. "Is anything broken? Where do you hurt?"

"Back . . . of my . . . head. My leg." Jennie bit her lip as another wave of pain hit. This one brought nausea. "I'm going to . . ." She turned over and threw up. She felt hot and sweaty and cold all at once. Jennie's agonizing groan faded into a spinning vortex as she hung on the edge of consciousness.

"Oh gross. She got barf on my shoe."

"Cool it, Brandy. It's not like she did it on purpose."

"I know, it's just . . . She isn't dead, is she?"

"No. Maybe she passed out."

Jennie opened her eyes again and tried to talk but managed only a muffled groan.

"She must have a concussion." Corisa sat back on her heels. "Her jeans are all bloody. I wonder what happened."

"Shouldn't we put a tourniquet on her leg or something?" Brandy shone the light on Jennie's leg.

"Um . . . looks like it stopped," Corisa said. "But, yeah, if we try to move her it might start bleeding again. I can't see very well, but it looks like something punctured it." She frowned. "Take off your T-shirt."

"Me? Why don't you take off yours?"

Corisa sighed and gave Brandy a look of disgust. "Because I'm not wearing one under my sweats and you are."

"Oh." Brandy handily slipped her arms inside her sweat shirt, wriggled around a bit, then pulled a white shirt through the neck hole and handed it to her sister. Corisa wrapped the shirt around Jennie's leg and tied it.

"We should get her back to the cabin." Brandy started to slide an arm under Jennie's head.

"Brandy, don't. We shouldn't move her."

"We can't just let her lie here all night."

"I know." Corisa ran a hand through her hair. "Let me think."

"What's your name?" Brandy asked.

"I . . ." Jennie frowned. She closed her eyes, trying to make her brain come up with an answer.

"Don't, Brandy. Can't you see she's in pain? We have to get help."

"How? We can't leave her alone."

"I know that, dummy. Why don't you and Lucy stay here. I'll go get the cell phone and call 9-1-1."

"You're not going to take the flashlight, are you?"

"I need it more than you do. I'll be right back."

"Bring a blanket," Brandy called after her. "We should cover her and keep her warm until the rescue guys get here."

"I will. And water."

"Stay here, girl." Brandy held the dog's collar, though Lucy didn't look like she was going anywhere.

The flashlight beam disappeared, leaving in its wake a creepy twilight. After several minutes the sky seemed lighter again.

"Thanks," Jennie murmured.

"Hey, no problem. It's just good that Lucy found you."

"Yeah."

"What happened to you anyway?" Brandy asked.

Jennie closed her eyes, letting her arm rest against her forehead. "Don't know," she rasped.

"I'm sorry. I shouldn't be making you talk."

"Hurts."

Lucy lay down beside Jennie, licking her hand. Jennie petted her. *Nice dog. Thanks.*

"My name is Brandy. My sister is Corisa," she repeated. "We live in Vancouver. She's the oldest, if you haven't already guessed. Most of the time she's nice, but she can get so-o-o bossy." Brandy sighed. "I'm fourteen. Corisa's sixteen. How old are. . . ? Oops. I wasn't going to ask you any more questions, was I? And I'm talking too much. I know I am. Mom and Dad are always saying that. Corisa calls me a motor mouth. But it's kind of scary out here and . . ." She laughed. "I shouldn't be scared. Not with Lucy here."

Lucy lifted her head. A low growl started in her belly and rose to her throat. She bolted to her feet and began barking furiously.

Brandy grabbed Jennie's hand. "There's something out there."

Jennie's reassurance fled. What if the coyotes had returned? Or worse. Corisa and Brandy had said she looked like someone had beaten her up. What if whoever had hurt her was coming back?

15

Lucy pattered across crisp leaves in a pacing rhythm as if she were circling them. At least she hoped it was Lucy. Jennie could see nothing but dark forms against a darker backdrop now.

A light bobbed through the woods again. "Hey, it's just me. Lucy, settle down."

Jennie had a feeling Corisa was the least of the dog's worries. Lucy kept barking. She gave one final warning, then came back to check on the girls. She'd apparently frightened away whatever—or whoever—had been out there.

"I couldn't find the phone," Corisa said. "Looked everywhere. You brought it, didn't you? I remember Dad handing it to you at the house."

"Of course."

"You didn't leave it in the car, did you? Dad will have to drive all the way back out here. He will not be hap—"

"Oh no," Brandy interrupted. "I left it in the garage. I set it down on some boxes to grab the cooler. I was gonna go back and get it, but—"

"Dad is going to go ballistic when he finds out we don't have it. And how are we going to call for help?"

"I'm sorry," Brandy sighed. "I didn't mean to."

"Okay, let's not panic. I'm sure Dad will know something is wrong when he calls and we don't answer."

"What are we going to do about . . . her?"

"We'll figure something out. But first we have to get her to the cabin. It's getting colder by the minute. I brought a couple of blankets. We'll put the heavy wool one under her. Did she tell you her name?"

"Not yet. It hurts her to talk."

It did hurt to talk, but that wasn't all. Jennie honestly didn't know how to answer their questions. As strange as it seemed, she had no idea how she'd ended up in the woods or how she'd been hurt. She couldn't tell them her name because she didn't know it.

"Did you bring the water?" Brandy asked. "That might help."

"Yeah, and a straw." Corisa sank to her knees and placed the straw in Jennie's mouth.

Jennie drew in several swallows. She'd never tasted anything so good in her life. Water dribbled out of her mouth, running along her jaw and into her hair. Jennie cleared her throat and murmured another thank-you.

"No problem." Looking Jennie over, a worried look crossed Corisa's face. "It might hurt when we move you, but we have to. Can't let you stay out here all night. It's supposed to get below freezing tonight. I'm worried about your neck, though. I mean, it could be broken."

"I don't think so," Jennie managed to tell them. "It hurts, but I can move everything."

"Okay, I guess we don't have much choice. We'll put these blankets under you and carry you to the house."

"You'll be comfortable there until we can get some help," Brandy said.

"Don't worry. We'll take care of you," Corisa added.

Jennie braced herself for the move, clenching her teeth when the pain came. Trying to hold her body without twisting, they rolled her onto her right side, then bunched the blanket against her back. They moved around to her back and carefully rolled Jennie over the lump of blanket and onto her left side. Moving her as little as possible, they straightened the blanket underneath her. With Corisa at her head and Brandy at her feet, they began the trek out of the woods. Twice they had to lay her back down and rest.

"We're almost there," Corisa told her. "I hope we're not hurting you too much."

"Not too bad," Jennie gasped. "Getting used to it."

But she wasn't. Every movement seemed worse than the last. Considering the alternative, though, Jennie wasn't about to complain. Anything was better than being out in the woods alone all night.

They eventually reached a clearing where a yard light spread out a welcoming aura.

When Jennie saw the three buildings she let out a sharp gasp and grabbed at the sides of the blanket. "Wait!" she panted. "Something's wrong."

"It's okay," Corisa reassured her. "You don't have to be afraid. This is our cabin. You'll be safe here."

"No—someone . . ." Jennie pinched her eyes shut. An image flitted in and out of her mind so quickly she couldn't grasp it. She only knew it was terrible. *What's wrong with me? I'm more scared here than I was in the woods.* She'd never been here before, yet there was something about it. Something terrifying.

"What's that?" A stained-glass window in the smallest of the buildings caught her eye.

Corisa and Brandy must have followed her gaze. They both laughed.

"That's our outhouse," Brandy explained. "When our parents first bought the land, we used to pitch a tent and camp out here. They decided they needed an outhouse. At first Dad just dug a pit and put some boards around it. By the next year we had a septic tank, a well, a real toilet, and a shower, and Mom made the stained-glass window for the door. Then Dad had to have a place for all his tools and equipment, so he built the shed. And now we have the house."

"Enough already," Corisa said, giving Jennie an apologetic glance.

Jennie's panic subsided as they neared the house and

the lighted windows. She was cold, and the cabin would be a warm and welcome relief.

There's nothing to be afraid of, Jennie told herself. *Like Corisa said, you're safe.* Only Jennie didn't feel safe. Not at all.

They entered the cabin, and Corisa again reassured Jennie. She bolted the door for extra security. Once the girls had placed Jennie in the bed in their parents' main-floor bedroom, the worst of Jennie's fears slipped away. She didn't understand why she'd reacted as she had. There was certainly nothing frightening about the place. In fact, it was one of the nicest cabins Jennie had ever seen. The girls had taken off the beige Matisse bedcover and pillow shams and covered the clean sheets with the blanket they'd brought her in on. Corisa piled several pillows behind Jennie's head.

Brandy came in with hot chocolates, and within a few minutes the questions started again.

After a couple sips of the wonderfully warm drink, Jennie tried to explain. "I wish I could answer you, but I don't remember."

"Not anything?" Brandy asked. "Not even your name?"

"Nothing."

"I wouldn't worry too much about that right now." Corisa set her cup on the nightstand. "You got a nasty bump on your head. Probably a concussion with temporary amnesia."

"Temporary amnesia?" Brandy repeated. "Like you'd really know. Quit acting like you're some kind of doctor."

"I'm not." Corisa folded her arms. "But I do know some things." Turning to Jennie she added, "I've had some first-aid classes, and I plan to go to medical school."

Brandy rested a hip on the end of the bed. "I've had first aid too." Her expression softened as she shifted her attention back to Jennie. "Do you think you have amnesia?"

"I don't know. Maybe."

Corisa bit her bottom lip. "Oh, Brandy, what a time for you to forget the phone. She really needs to be in the hospital."

"I said I was sorry."

"I wish there was some way to get you out of here." Corisa tipped her head back.

"Don't you have a car?" Jennie didn't remember seeing one when they came in.

"No. Dad dropped us off. He and Mom will be back in a couple days."

"We have our bikes," Brandy said. "Maybe one of us could go out to the main road and flag down a car."

"Good idea, but not tonight. It's too far. We can't risk it."

Brandy got off the bed and began pacing. "I wish there was something we could do now."

"I guess I could try to make it out tonight," Corisa offered. "I'd have to rig some kind of light on my bike. I should be able to reach the ranger station within a couple of hours."

"How far is it?" Jennie asked.

"About fifteen miles."

"You're right. That's too far." Jennie put her hand on Corisa's arm. "I'll be okay. My head feels better already."

Relief flooded Corisa's gray eyes. "Are you sure?"

"Yeah. I'd probably get a worse headache worrying about you. Besides, you said your dad might be coming back when he realizes you don't have the phone."

"Right. He could even be out tonight." Brandy frowned. "Of course, if he's working on a project, he might not even call tonight. He's an architect."

"It doesn't matter." Corisa sounded more sure of herself now. "I can ride out first thing in the morning. Once I get to the main road, I should easily be able to find someone to help us."

With that settled, Jennie closed her eyes. The warm room and hot chocolate made her sleepy. "Sorry. I'm really tired."

"Guess we should let you rest." Corisa's gaze traveled from Jennie's head to her jacket and lingered there a moment. She seemed puzzled about something. Finally she focused on the white T-shirt still tied around Jennie's leg. "First, though, I think we should clean you up and look at your leg. We should put something on it so it doesn't get infected."

When they went to help Jennie remove her jeans, she stopped them. "I think you should cut them off."

"Like they do on *ER*." Brandy nodded. "Good idea. I'll get some scissors."

"A couple of towels too," Jennie said. "The material is plastered to my skin. When you pull it off, the scab will come, too, and it'll start bleeding again."

Corisa gave her an odd look. "You sound like you've had experience with this sort of thing."

Jennie frowned. "I don't know . . . maybe."

"I'll get the first-aid kit." For a moment Corisa looked as if she didn't quite believe her; then she shrugged and left the room.

Several minutes later Jennie's torn jeans had been cut away and towels had been placed under her leg. Jennie gritted her teeth and held on to the bedclothes while Corisa eased off the square of material still attached to the wound on Jennie's thigh.

"Just pull it off," Jennie begged. Hot, searing pain ripped through her as they gave it a final yank.

"She was right. It's bleeding again."

"Put pressure on it," Jennie hissed.

"I am." Corisa pressed a clean towel over it.

When the bleeding stopped and Corisa removed the towel, Jennie got her first real look at the wound. It looked as though something had sliced through the side of her leg, taking out about an inch-wide chunk. "I've been shot."

"You . . . you're kidding, r-right?" Brandy stammered.

"Are you remembering what happened?" Corisa tucked the bloodied towel against Jennie's outer thigh.

"No." Jennie drew her hands down her face. Tears gathered in her eyes. "I just know."

"Please don't cry." Brandy touched her shoulder. "It'll be okay."

Corisa smiled. "Right. Dad might be on his way out here. Maybe he called and realizes we don't have the cell phone. If he thinks we're in trouble he'll either come out himself or send the ranger or one of the neighbors to check on us."

"We'll take care of you until then. I'll bet by tomorrow you'll feel better and be able to remember everything."

"M-maybe it won't be as bad as it looks." Corisa's words and the worry in her eyes didn't match. She opened the bottle of hydrogen peroxide she'd brought in. "This is gonna hurt."

"I know, but it'll kill the germs. Go ahead." Jennie tipped her head back and braced herself for the burning pain. The clear liquid bubbled white as it hit her wound and soaked into the towel. Corisa kept apologizing as she used a sterile gauze to mop up the excess fluid and finished putting a dressing on it.

Once they'd gotten Jennie cleaned up and into a pair of Corissa's pajamas, the girls shut off the bedroom light and closed the door, leaving Jennie alone to rest, promising to check on her every couple of hours during the night.

The partially closed blinds allowed just enough light into the room to take the edge off the darkness. Jennie began to relax. Her head ached, but not as severely. Maybe Brandy and Corisa were right. After a good night's sleep, she'd feel better.

Jennie had almost fallen asleep when she heard footsteps outside. She opened her eyes as a shadow figure passed by the bedroom window.

16

Jennie awoke the next morning to the sound of birds twittering in trees outside the bedroom window. Sun streamed in between the slats in the white miniblinds, leaving warm golden stripes on the ivory walls.

Remnants of an odd dream hung like cobwebs in her mind. She'd been running from something . . . and had fallen. Instead of landing, the fall went on and on. Her heart still hammered with the fear of being caught by . . . What? Whom? Jennie still had no idea.

She heard voices coming from another part of the cabin. Corissa and Brandy. Memories of her rescue and Lucy, the wonderful dog who'd saved her life, flooded into her consciousness. If it hadn't been for them, she doubted she'd have survived the night. She smiled, thinking about how frightened she'd been the night before when she'd heard the footsteps and seen the shadow outside the bedroom window. At first she'd been terrified, thinking someone was after her. Turned out to be Brandy taking Lucy outside for a walk.

Jennie felt better this morning. Less frightened, less pain—slightly. Her leg and head still hurt, but not quite as much as they had when she'd awakened in the woods.

"Do you really think she has amnesia?" Jennie heard Brandy ask.

"Either that or she's lying. The coat she had on when we found her is definitely Mom's. Mom and Dad left their old ones in the closet last time we were here. Remember?"

"Yeah. And last night when we brought her in, she acted like she'd been here before."

"She was scared," Corisa added. "You could see it in her eyes."

"Which makes me wonder if . . . ."

Jennie tuned them out, focusing on Corisa's strange remark. She'd been wearing their mother's jacket? She sank both hands into her snarled and matted hair. They thought she might be lying. Maybe she was. She had no way of knowing. There had been something familiar about the place, frighteningly so. But Jennie couldn't remember ever having been there. The girls were right; she had been filled with a sense of panic the moment she saw the place. How had she gotten the coat? Who had beaten her up? Why couldn't she remember? So many questions. No answers. Not a single one.

Jennie eased off the covers and dangled her legs over the edge of the bed, slowly raising herself into a sitting position. Dizziness almost forced her back down. But she needed to get up. Needed some answers.

The bedroom door opened. Corisa came in with a tray. "What are you doing?" She set the tray on the bed. "You shouldn't be getting out of bed. Not without help."

"I heard you talking and . . . the jacket . . . I didn't know."

"We figured that."

"Oh?"

"Well, obviously you've been in the cabin. Someone beat you up and maybe shot you in the leg. Leaving you out in the woods like that . . . they must not have wanted you to survive. Are you sure you don't remember anything?"

"You think I'm lying, don't you? I heard you talking."

"No. Brandy and I both believe you. You have an honest face—black-and-blue, but honest. You can tell a lot by looking into people's eyes, you know."

"Thanks." When Jennie tried to stand, she felt sweaty

and chilled at the same time. The room began to spin. "I think I'm going to faint again."

Corisa grabbed her arm and directed her back into bed. Brandy held a cool, wet washcloth to her forehead, and after several minutes the dizziness passed. Eventually, Jennie managed to choke down the dry cereal, milk, and toast Corisa had brought for breakfast.

Corisa opened the blinds, revealing a perfect view of the river. A light snowfall had softly blanketed the countryside.

"Wow. It's gorgeous." Jennie squinted as the sun poured in through the window.

"I love being in the mountains when it snows." Corisa sat on the edge of the bed.

"I can see why." Jennie set the tray aside and leaned back against the pillows. "Guess you won't be able to go for help. Snow is beautiful to look at but not great for bike riding."

"Not a problem. I can get good traction on the gravel road. Might slow me down some, but I should be able to reach the ranger station in two hours."

"Um . . ." Brandy came in carrying a stack of clothing. "I'm not so sure you should go, Corisa."

"It'll be fine. Sun's shining. The snow will probably melt by the time I reach the main road." She grinned. "Now quit worrying."

Brandy shrugged. "Whatever." Glancing at Jennie she said, "We washed your clothes last night. But your jeans . . ."

"We had to toss them." Corisa grabbed the stack of clothes. "I found some sweats with a drawstring that will probably fit. They'll be a little short, but—"

"They'll be fine. I'm not that much taller than you."

"When you feel like it, we can help you get dressed." She frowned. "You'll probably need to go to the bathroom."

Jennie nodded. "I do, but I'm not sure I can make it that far."

"No problem. We have a Porta-Potty."

"A what?"

"A portable toilet." Brandy giggled. "It's for nighttime and emergencies. The rule is, if you use it, you empty it and clean it up for the next person."

Corisa rolled her eyes. "You make it sound so gross." Turning to Jennie she said, "You won't have to clean it. Brandy will."

"Me! No way . . ."

"Just hush and get it, okay?"

Brandy mumbled and left the room, coming back within a few minutes with a white plastic-lidded container. Jennie managed to get up and use it without fainting. When she'd finished, Brandy and Corisa helped her wash up, brush her hair, and get dressed.

"Want us to help you into the living room?" Corisa tightened the drawstring on the loose navy sweats and tied them.

"Please." She nodded. The workout had exhausted her. She probably should have stayed in the bed, but she didn't want to be alone. Jennie put an arm around each of their necks and limped into the spacious living room. Again she felt a twinge of recognition. Another lightning-fast image of forms—people without faces.

"Are you okay?" Corisa asked.

"I . . ." Jennie couldn't finish. "Yeah. I had some kind of flashback."

"Maybe your memory is coming back."

"I hope so."

Once they'd settled her on the couch, Corisa went upstairs and Brandy went back into the bedroom for pillows. Corisa returned carrying a sweater and a large fleece blanket. Tucking the blanket around Jennie, she said, "This should keep you warm and cozy."

"Thanks." Jennie leaned forward while Brandy fluffed and positioned the pillows.

"There. Now you can relax."

"After all that I need a nap." Jennie leaned back, thankful to be lying down again. Corisa pulled a bulky blue sweater over her head and opened the closet for her coat and mittens.

"I don't want you to go, Cor." Brandy clasped her hands in front of her. "I'm scared. What if whoever was using the cabin and hurt her comes back?"

"They won't."

Brandy sighed. "You don't know that."

Corisa grunted. "Come on, Brandy. Don't be a baby. She needs medical help. You know that as well as I do. Besides, I'll be back before you know it."

Jennie closed her eyes, too tired to argue either way. She did need medical care. She'd barely been able to walk into the living room. The wound in her leg throbbed, and her head felt as though it had been wedged in a vise. As Corisa stepped outside, Jennie offered a silent prayer for safety and success.

By eight-thirty Corisa was on her way. She would bike to the main road and head toward the ranger station, which was the most likely place to find help.

An hour later Corisa was back, walking her bike and looking flushed, tired, and seriously annoyed. "Can you believe it? The tire went flat about three miles down the road." She stepped onto the porch and stomped snow off her shiny black boots.

"You want to take my bike?" Brandy asked.

"That *was* your bike. Both the tires on mine are flat." She pulled a ragged wool mitten off one hand and wiggled her red fingers. "I was going to try to walk to the main road, but it's freezing out there. We'll have to wait until the snow melts or Dad shows up."

"I'll bet that's why he isn't here yet." Brandy stepped back to let her sister inside. "The roads are probably closed."

Corisa peeled off her ski jacket and sweater, then pushed up the sleeves of her red turtleneck. "I feel terrible."

"You did your best," Jennie offered.

"That's not good enough." Corisa hung her jacket over

a chair, poured herself a glass of water, and offered some to Jennie. "You need to see a doctor. What if you have a concussion or something really serious wrong with you?"

"At least she's not getting worse." Brandy dropped to the floor and sat cross-legged on the woven area rug. "Maybe while we're waiting for Dad, we can help solve your mystery."

"You mean help me remember?" Jennie concentrated on Brandy's blurred face, trying to bring it into focus. Blurred vision, headache, sleepiness. She was getting worse but didn't want the girls to worry.

"Partly," Brandy answered. "Okay, we find you in the woods wearing Mom's coat. You have no identification. While you were sleeping this morning, I took Lucy and went back to where we found you. I thought maybe I'd find a clue—like maybe a backpack or camping gear." She shrugged. "I walked all around. There's nothing."

Corisa eyed the closet. "We know you were in the cabin; otherwise how could you have gotten Mom's jacket?"

"And Dad's jacket was on the floor in the closet bunched up in the corner. There were some bread crumbs on the floor like someone had eaten in there. Corisa and I think you might have been kept in there by a kidnapper or something. I mean, nobody would eat or sleep in the closet unless they had to."

"That sounds awful." Jennie glanced from one to the other.

"I read about these people once—" Brandy paused. "They were really mean to their kids. They'd beat them up and put them in closets and stuff."

"You think my parents might have done this to me?" Jennie shuddered at the thought. She searched her mind for family members but only came up with a dark, gaping hole. "I'm sorry. I can't . . ."

"Remember? I know. Anyway, we found some scuff marks on the floor." Brandy got up and crouched in front of the open closet. "Looks like something heavy was shoved up against the door, like the sofa."

Corisa reached into one of the kitchen cupboards and brought out a popper and bag of popcorn. "That is so lame. I doubt it was her parents. For one thing, why would they bring her clear up here? To our cabin? Personally, I think she was kidnapped."

"Yeah," Brandy agreed. "This would be a great place to hide you until they got the ransom. Are you rich? Maybe there's a reward for finding you." Grinning, she added, "Cor and I could split it."

"Get real, Brandy."

Jennie closed her eyes. It hurt to think. "If I was kidnapped, wouldn't there be something on the news? You know how they show pictures of missing people. Or maybe the radio."

"We don't have a radio or a TV." Brandy made a face. "We don't even have a CD player. Just the cell phone—and we left that at home."

"If only we had a way out."

Corisa gave her sister a dirty look. "If only you hadn't forgotten the phone."

Brandy got up and looked out the window. "You don't have to rub it in."

"I may be dense," Jennie said, "but what are you two doing here all alone?"

"I suppose it does seem strange." Corisa poured oil and popcorn into the popper. "It's sort of hard to explain."

"Not really." Brandy came back and perched on the arm of the couch. "The thing is, twice a year, spring and fall, our parents bring us up here for a kind of wilderness experience."

"Why?"

"Because Brandy is always arguing—"

"Me! You always blame me. Just because I'm the youngest."

"See," Corisa went on, "we fight a lot. I mean, all brothers and sisters fight, don't they? But Mom hates it."

Jennie wondered if she had a brother or sister and if they fought.

"About three years ago," Brandy picked up the story, "Mom got so mad she decided we needed to learn to appreciate each other. First she made us camp out in the backyard. We couldn't even have friends over. 'You'll have fun,' she said. She and her sister used to go camping together and they got along well, so she thinks it will work for us. We're, like, supposed to 'bond,' you know?"

"Dad wasn't too thrilled with the idea of our coming out here, but he goes along with it," Corisa interjected. "*Only* because we learned first aid and survival skills *and* take a cell phone with us." Corisa glared at her sister. "Of course, Miss Brainless here blew that one."

Brandy ignored her. "Now they both think a few days out here without our friends or any of our trappings will build character."

"Trappings?"

"That's what they call our CD players and stuff we like doing. They want to give us a chance to get back to nature," Brandy huffed.

"Mostly we're supposed to learn to get along better."

"Is it working? Does it make you any closer?" *Apparently it hasn't.* Jennie kept her thoughts to herself.

Corisa shrugged. "We get kind of bored. We're not even allowed to call anyone except Mom or Dad, and then only if there's a problem." Another dark glare.

Brandy pursed her lips. "Sometimes I think it does help. We've learned how to rely on each other."

"And we always end up having a good time."

Jennie's head was reeling. She tried to pay attention, but the conversation kept drifting into nonsense. "It's a long way from the backyard to this . . . wilderness. Seems kind of extreme to leave you all alone out here."

"Mom says it's safer than leaving us alone in town, and they do that a lot. We've been coming to the cabin for years. It's totally safe. . . ." Corisa swallowed hard. "At least it always has been."

"Hey, maybe there's a bright side to this. Once Mom and Dad find out someone's been staying here, they won't make us hang out together anymore."

"Yeah, maybe." Neither of the girls looked especially cheered by the thought.

Jennie glanced outside. The snow had begun to melt under a now hazy sun.

Brandy got up and paced across the room and back. "I wish Dad would get here. The main roads must be plowed by now. What if something happened to him? Like an accident or—"

"Relax, Brandy. I'm sure he'll be here soon."

"I hope so." She came back to the sofa and settled a suspicious gaze on Jennie. "Are you sure you can't remember your name?"

"No clue." Jennie sighed.

Brandy planted her fists against her hips. "Then we'll have to give you one. We can't keep calling you 'she' and 'her.' "

Brandy examined Jennie's face. "You look sort of like our cousin Brittany. She's tall and thin like you, and her hair's about the same length and color. Her eyes are lighter blue, but . . ."

Brandy wrapped her arms around herself. "Brittany. That sound okay to you?"

"I guess."

Brandy nodded and looked out the window again. "What if you were kidnapped, Brittany? What happened to the kidnappers? What if they come back?"

"They probably won't," Corisa answered.

"How do you know?"

"I don't for sure." Corisa put an arm around her sister's shoulders. "I'll bet he got the ransom money and decided not to give her back. They probably think she's dead."

"Well, what if they're out in the woods looking for her?"

"Brandy, calm down. We'll be fine."

Jennie slid her legs off the couch and started to stand. She still felt light-headed. "I need to use the bathroom."

"In or out?" Brandy asked.

"Out. Maybe some fresh air will wake me up."

Halfway to the outhouse Jennie had second thoughts. She felt a heavy weight on her back. Face down in the dirt. Couldn't breathe. In an instant the image was gone, leaving Jennie breathless and perspiring. She stumbled and would have fallen if Brandy and Corisa hadn't been holding her up.

They had just reached the outhouse when Lucy started barking. Jennie heard the distant hum of an engine and tires crunching on the gravel road.

"They're coming back." Jennie's pulse pounded in her head. "Quick. We've got to hide."

17

Corisa and Brandy propped Jennie against the back of the outhouse. As soon as they let her go she sank to the ground. Perspiration clung to her upper lip and forehead. She'd cautioned them to leave her and run into the woods while they had a chance, but they hadn't listened.

She didn't quite understand why she was reacting in such a frantic way to the approaching car. All she knew was that someone had nearly killed her and she didn't know who. Jennie was almost afraid to remember anything. What if whoever had left her for dead was someone she knew?

They'd brought her here to this cabin. It could have been someone who knew Brandy and Corisa.

The girls stood watch on either side of her, peering around the corner, waiting for the vehicle to come into sight.

"It's Dad!" The words came out in a swish as Brandy stepped from her hiding place and ran into the yard.

Corisa slipped her arm under Jennie's and helped her up. "You'll be okay now. We'll get you to a hospital."

A sudden, terrifying thought slammed into Jennie's head. What if their father was the one who'd brought her here?

Her fears were partially allayed as she watched the man emerge from the car and pull Brandy into his arms.

"Dad, I am so glad you came back. Did you find the phone?"

"You didn't bring it?" He closed the car door and ran a hand through his thick black hair, making it stand on end. "Honey, you know better."

Brandy explained what she'd done.

Adjusting his glasses he said, "No wonder you didn't answer. You had me so worried. I headed out last night, but the state patrol stopped me just out of Cougar. I had to spend the night in a hotel and wait for the roads to open."

"We knew you would come eventually." Brandy looped an arm through his and dragged him forward. "We really needed the phone this time. We found this girl—"

"Girl? What girl?" Their father's gaze shot to Jennie and Corisa.

"Good grief. What happened?"

"We don't know for sure. Brittany . . . Well, that's not really her name. We gave it to her. Lucy found her in the woods last night, and we brought her here," Brandy explained. "She's hurt really bad. Corisa thinks she has a concussion. Somebody beat her up and shot her in the leg. If we hadn't found her she'd probably be dead. . . ."

"Whoa. Slow down." His expression was one of concern as he looked Jennie over. "Maybe we'd better get her into the house. She doesn't look like she should be walking around." Taking his cell phone out of the car, he called the authorities and gave them directions. He handed Brandy the phone and helped Corisa take Jennie back inside. "While we're waiting I want you to tell me exactly what happened."

Once they'd made Jennie comfortable on the couch and the girls had explained how they found their mystery girl in the woods, Mr. Graham brought in a chair from the dining area and set it next to Jennie. He leaned toward her, placed his fingers under her jaw, and tilted her face up to the light. Frown lines etched his forehead as he scrutinized her face. Moving back, he rested his elbows on his knees. "What's your name, honey? Who did this to you?"

"She doesn't know, Dad," Brandy answered for her. "She doesn't remember who she is or how she got hurt or anything."

He hushed Brandy and turned back to Jennie. "Is that true?"

Jennie glanced up at him and nodded. She bit into her lower lip.

"Well . . ." He patted her hand. "I'm not absolutely certain, but I think I can clear up at least part of the mystery." He stood and walked to the door. "I need to get something out of the car."

Seconds later he was back in the chair holding up a newspaper for all the girls to see. "With the bruises on your face, it's a little hard to tell, but the hair and eyes . . . I think you might be the girl who's been missing since Saturday morning. Does the name Jennie McGrady sound familiar to you?"

Jennie looked at the color photo of an attractive girl with long, dark hair. She had a wide smile that reached her dark blue eyes. In another photo the same girl sat on a sofa holding a little boy named Nick—her brother. The parents stood behind them. They looked a lot alike—the boy, Jennie McGrady, and their father. The mother was pretty with shoulder-length auburn hair. They looked happy. For a moment, she wished she *could* be the girl in the paper.

She stared at Jennie McGrady for a long time, wishing she could tell Mr. Graham he was right. Instead, she sighed and handed the paper back to him. "I don't know them. I've never seen them before."

"Hmm. I was hoping that seeing familiar faces might trigger something. Maybe you're this missing girl. Maybe not. Jennie McGrady was last seen near Battle Ground driving a red Mustang. They haven't located her car yet. She was supposed to rendezvous with some friends at the Lewis River Campground. That's quite a ways from here. But if she got lost and made a wrong turn, she could have ended up out here. The authorities suspect her car went off the road. It's possible you had an accident and walked out."

"But, Dad, what about her leg—where she was shot? And the bruises." Brandy brushed her hair out of her face.

"She was shot?"

"On her leg. Right, Brittany?"

Jennie nodded and pointed to the area of the wound.

"We don't know for sure it was a gunshot, Brandy."

Corisa stole a glance at Jennie.

"Brittany said it was."

"I wonder why you'd think that. Do you remember being shot at?" Mr. Graham examined Jennie's face.

Jennie shook her head. "No. It's hard to explain. I know things, but . . . Corisa's right. I could have hurt it on a tree limb, or . . . or something. It's just that when I saw it, that was the first thing I thought of."

"I'm certainly no expert on this sort of thing." He rubbed his clean-shaven jaw. "We'll just have to wait until a doctor has a look at you and the authorities can put together some clues. If someone was holding you here, there are probably prints. With all the new equipment available to them these days, they'll have it figured out in no time."

"I hope so." Jennie pulled her heavy hair into a ponytail, then let it fall back around her shoulders. She needed a shower badly.

"You do look like her." Corisa peered at the picture in the paper, then at Jennie. "Jennie is sixteen and lives in Portland." Her gaze dropped back to the paper. "Wow, if this is you, you're famous. It says you're like a real-life Nancy Drew, always helping police solve crimes."

Brandy read over her sister's shoulder. "I wonder if you were working on a case and that's why you got shot."

"Girls," their dad cautioned, "enough with the speculation. We'll find out soon enough." He slapped his knees and stood up. "Now, how about some lunch?"

Within the hour, the place was crawling with deputies, and two emergency medical technicians, Dan and Linda, checked her over. Even though she'd been up and walking, they insisted on stabilizing her neck and putting her on a stretcher. While Linda started an IV, Dan hung a bag of fluid. They soon had her strapped onto the stretcher and out the door.

While they worked, a uniformed officer, who'd introduced himself as Deputy Ross with the sheriff's department, asked all kinds of questions Jennie couldn't answer. Who had beat her up? What was she doing in the woods? Why had she been in the house? When had she come and how?

All she could tell him was that she'd awakened in the woods, wearing Mrs. Graham's jacket. Only she hadn't known that until Corisa and Brandy had told her. She felt like a specimen under a microscope and wasn't sure how much more she could handle. The pain in her head seemed to be worsening again.

"Sheriff, can't these questions wait? At least hold off until she's seen a physician."

Deputy Ross seemed annoyed by Mr. Graham's insistence but didn't argue. He gave Jennie an I'll-deal-with-you-later look, then in a kind voice that didn't meet the sternness in his eyes, said, "That may be for the best. I'll take your statement later this afternoon. Don't think about leaving town."

Jennie groaned. "I don't even know who I am. How would I know where to go?"

His lips curled into a half smile. "You have a point there—providing you're telling me the truth."

Jennie wished there was something she could say to reassure him. She doubted anything would.

To the EMTs, Deputy Ross said, "Go ahead and take her in. Make sure they don't release her until I've had a chance to talk to her."

"You got it." When the deputy left, Dan rolled his eyes and mumbled something under his breath.

Just as the EMTs were putting her into the ambulance, a beige Oldsmobile tore into the driveway. A middle-aged man climbed out and jogged toward them. As he got closer she recognized him as the man she'd seen in the newspaper photo—Jennie McGrady's father. He was tall and handsome despite the jagged scar on his jaw.

"Jennie, thank God. I came as soon as I . . ." He came to within a foot of them and stopped. Questions filled his dark blue eyes. He closed them briefly, taking in a sharp breath.

Jennie pulled her hand away when he reached for it.

Mr. Graham stepped between him and Jennie as if to protect her. "Who are you?"

"Detective McGrady, Homicide—Portland Police. I'm her father. The sheriff's office called me as soon as they got your call." He focused back on Jennie, a helpless look in his eyes. "Princess, it's me."

Jennie shook her head. Pain coursed through her head with such intensity she could barely hear her own cry.

"Please. You're upsetting her." Mr. Graham led the man away. "I'm sorry, Detective McGrady, but are you sure this is your daughter? She doesn't seem to know you. I'll admit there's a resemblance, but with all those facial injuries . . ."

"She's my daughter, all right. No question."

Jennie couldn't hear any more. Linda climbed up beside her, and Dan started to close the doors.

"Wait!" Mr. McGrady yanked the door out of Dan's hands. The medic and Mr. Graham held him when he started to get into the ambulance. "I need to talk to her for just a minute. Please."

They dropped his arms, and for a moment Jennie was afraid he'd come inside. He didn't. "I'm not going to hurt you, princess. Don't be frightened. Mr. Graham tells me you might have amnesia. It's all right if you can't remember. For now it's enough for you to know you have a family who loves you. I'm going back to pick up your mother right now. We'll see you at the hospital."

Jennie didn't respond.

Mr. McGrady patted Dan's back. "Take good care of my little girl."

"We sure will, sir."

The back doors of the ambulance closed, shutting her away from the man who claimed to be her father. Even with the doors and her eyes tightly shut she couldn't wipe away the image of his face—the hurt in his eyes, his surprise when she'd pulled away from him.

You have family.

They love you. He called you princess. His little girl.

Could he really be her father? Could she be the missing girl? This Jennie McGrady?

The rescue unit began backing up, warning anyone in their way with its *beep-beep-beep*. Linda adjusted the drip on the IV and took her blood pressure.

When Linda had finished taking her vital signs, Jennie covered her eyes with her hands, trying to keep her tears at bay. But sobs still tore loose from the back of her throat, and she wasn't sure why.

"Hey, it's going to be all right." The EMT touched her shoulder in a reassuring gesture. "We'll take good care of you."

But was it going to be okay? All during the drive in she tried to find remnants of what or who she might have been prior to waking up in the woods the night before. The man with the scar seemed positive she was his daughter. But how could he be so sure?

She'd seen her face in a mirror that morning and couldn't see much resemblance. Her face was one big bruise with a jaw the size of a grapefruit. The puffy dark circles under her eyes made her look as if she'd spent an hour in the boxing ring with a prizefighter. She had scabs and open sores around her mouth. Her hair and her eyes might be a similar color to his, but if she was this McGrady person, wouldn't she remember something?

Maybe he was her father. If he truly was her dad, wouldn't she have felt something for him? Some kind of attachment? A memory? Instead of love, she felt fear. Instead of welcoming his touch, she'd pulled away. Jennie had no idea why he frightened her so. Why he still did.

Another questioned niggled at Jennie. How could Detective McGrady have known it was his daughter at the cabin? He'd gotten a call from the sheriff. Had he assumed it was her? Or had he known she was there because it was he who'd left her to die? Maybe he wasn't her father at all, but a kidnapper pretending to be her father so he could take her away and make certain she didn't escape a second time.

18

Jennie placed her arm over her eyes trying to still her wild imaginings. She wasn't being fair to the man. He'd shown genuine concern for her.

You were afraid of Mr. Graham, too, at first. Are you going to be afraid of everyone from now on?

Unless she'd been dropped on earth by an alien spaceship, she had family out there. People who loved her as Detective McGrady had said. But did they really love her? How could she know whom to trust? The black hole in her mind threatened to swallow her up.

Maybe this is all a wild dream, and you'll wake up to find it never happened. With that in mind, Jennie focused on the colors behind her closed eyelids until she fell asleep.

Something soft brushed against her cheek. Palm trees waved in the tropical breeze. Water lapped against a sandy shore. A dolphin jumped out of the water to snatch a fish she held out for him, then challenged her to a race. The image of a dark-haired guy with green eyes drifted into her thoughts and out again. Jennie clung to the image, begging it to stay. Disappointed, she opened her eyes.

No palm trees, no cute guy with green eyes, and no dolphins. Only the inside of an ambulance.

"Hey, sleepyhead." The EMT touched her arm. "How are you holding up?"

"Okay, I guess."

"We're at the hospital," Linda said. "Soon as we get the

doors open, we'll be wheeling you into the ER."

Jennie tried to recall the tropical images. There had been something tangible and familiar about them. Had she been there once? Had the dolphin and the guy with the green eyes emerged from the black hole? Could her memory be coming back?

She tucked away the pleasant thought and looked around at her new surroundings. Jennie felt strangely comfortable in the cool, sterile room Linda and Dan wheeled her into. After an RN checked her in, the EMTs and a couple hospital staff in surgical scrubs transferred her onto another stretcher.

Linda continued to give the nurses their report about Jennie. At the end she said, "We still need a positive ID, but there was a guy at the scene who says she's his daughter. If he's right, she's the kid that's been missing since Saturday morning—Jennie McGrady. Detective McGrady and his wife should be coming in any time."

Dan handed one of the women a business card. "You can reach Detective McGrady on his cell phone."

"Got it." She smiled down at Jennie. "I gotta tell you, you're one lucky girl."

Lucky? Jennie mumbled some kind of affirmation, then suffered through the humiliation of being stripped and put in a hospital gown. She'd barely gotten her arms into the sleeves when a woman came in introducing herself as Dr. Blackwell, the attending physician in the ER.

After the exam and several tests, Dr. Blackwell affirmed what Jennie already knew: She'd suffered a severe head trauma, which had apparently caused memory loss. The doctor also determined that the wound on her leg had been caused by a bullet. She'd called a neurosurgeon who'd be in shortly to determine the extent of the head injury, and had ordered a CT scan. "I discovered something else. Good news. You really are Jennie McGrady. We were able to get a positive ID by checking your X rays against the files we have. You had a healed fracture on your right arm from several months ago. They're a match." She glanced at the closed curtains. "There are some people out there who are extremely anxious to see you. Are you up to visitors?"

Jennie bit the corner of her lower lip. "I guess I should be, but . . ."

"It's okay. If you'd rather wait, we can get you admitted and I can order one visitor at a time. I've already told them that having you see all of them at once might be overwhelming."

"All of them? How many are there?"

"At least a dozen. I think some of them might be friends. They won't be thrilled, but it won't hurt them to wait until you're ready."

Jennie nodded. A dozen people. She cringed at the thought. Right now the prospect of seeing even one nearly sent her into a panic. What if one of them had beaten and shot her?

Dr. Blackwell touched her arm. "I think it might be a good idea if you saw your mother and father, though. Your mother especially. She's pregnant, and the way she's been pacing—"

"Pregnant? Aren't I a little old to have a pregnant mother?"

"You're only sixteen." Dr. Blackwell grinned. "From what I can tell, Jennie, you have a wonderful family. How about it?"

"Sure." Jennie sucked in a deep breath to straighten the knots in her stomach. "I guess."

The woman Jennie had seen in the newspaper came in first. *Susan,* the caption under the photo had read. *Susan McGrady.* She was prettier in person than in the photo. *Hi, Mom. Hi, Dad.* Jennie knew she should say it—or something like it—but the words caught in her throat.

Mrs. McGrady's eyes filled with tears. "Hi, sweetheart." She bent to kiss Jennie's cheek.

Jennie flinched despite her efforts not to.

Susan looked as if Jennie had slapped her. "Oh, honey, I . . ." She covered her mouth and closed her eyes, sinking into the chair one of the nurses had placed beside the stretcher. "I'm sorry. I can't seem to stop blubbering. It's just that I'm so happy to see you and so . . . thankful."

She pulled a tissue out of her jacket pocket, mopped her tears and blew her nose, then got up to throw it away. When she came back to the stretcher she seemed more composed. "It's going to be all right, sweetheart. Your dad says you don't remember anything. I'm sure you will in time. We just need to be patient." She looked at the curtain. "It seems so strange not to have you know me. Guess I shouldn't have tried to kiss you yet, but you're my little girl." Her shoulders raised and lowered in a long sigh. "Everyone's praying for you."

The curtain opened and Detective McGrady came in. Approaching them, he placed an arm around his wife and took hold of Jennie's hand. "They're wanting to transfer you upstairs. We'll talk more up there, okay?"

Jennie nodded. Seeing him again reassured her. *He has kind eyes. So does your mom.*

You can trust them, something inside promised.

"Are you really my parents?"

"Oh yes," Susan McGrady said. "And we love you more than you can imagine."

Jennie felt her cracked lips raise slightly at the corners. Her eyes drifted closed.

"Honey, we should go," Detective McGrady said.

Susan squeezed Jennie's hand. "The doctor said we shouldn't overwhelm you, so we won't. I just needed to see for myself . . ." The tears started again. "Oh, honey, I'm so sorry you were hurt. I should never have let you go up there alone. It's all my fault."

Jennie wished she could offer words of comfort, but she had nothing to give. She tried to open her eyes, but they felt leaden. "I'm tired," she mumbled. "So tired."

"Just rest, princess," her father said. "We'll be here when you wake up."

The curtains swished back and forth, leaving Jennie alone. In one way she welcomed the isolation. In another she felt oddly abandoned. Giving in to the weariness, she slipped once again into the dark recesses of her mind and hovered there.

———————

"How come she's been sleeping so long?" a child's voice penetrated Jennie's darkness.

"She's in a coma, sweetheart," a woman answered. "It happens sometimes when people have a brain injury."

"How did she get hurt?"

"We don't know for sure. The doctor thinks she fell and hit her head on a log."

"That musta hurt, huh? When's she gonna wake up?"

"I don't know. Soon, I hope." There was a catch in her throat. And the voice had a familiar feel to it. A picture of Susan McGrady floated into Jennie's mind. Her mother. *Mom*. It felt good somehow to think of her that way.

"But she's been asleep for two whole days."

"I know." Mom sighed. "You can talk to her if you want. The doctor says she might be able to hear us."

Two days. She must have lost consciousness in the emergency room. She remembered being alone after seeing her parents.

"Wake up, Jennie. I been waiting for you. Me and Mommy and Daddy and Lisa and Kurt and Aunt Kate and Uncle Kevin and Gram and Papa and Ryan and Scott and . . ." He paused for a breath. "And a whole bunch of your friends. I want you to wake up 'cause I miss you. Mommy and Daddy said you don't remember 'em, but you gotta 'member me 'cause I'm your brother."

"Tell her your name," Mom urged. "And how old you are."

"She'll know, won't she?"

"Maybe, but just in case."

"Okay." He touched her arm. "Hi, Jennie. I'm Nick and I'm five years old. You gotta wake up so's you can read to me again. Mama reads to me, but she doesn't do it as good as you."

Susan chuckled softly.

"How's it going?" a male voice interrupted him.

Detective McGrady. Dad.

"I'm talking to Jennie. Mom says she can hear me."

Jennie visualized the picture she'd seen of the McGrady family, bringing the little boy into focus. Even though she didn't have a tangible memory of him, she would have to pretend she did so she wouldn't hurt him as she had her parents. He sounded sweet, and judging from the way he talked he and his sister were close. What was his name again? *Nick.*

She felt heavy and dull. Like she'd been glued to the bed. She lifted her arm, surprised that it moved. Her eyes drifted open.

Susan McGrady was looking up at her husband, holding his hand as he kissed her full on the lips. They seemed oblivious to anyone but each other. Something inside her resonated approval.

They haven't always been like that. The thought surprised her. Was she beginning to remember? An image of her as a child riding in the car drifted through her mind. They were angry and fighting over something. The memory slipped away before Jennie could examine it.

Nick sat on Susan's lap. His eyes widened when he saw Jennie looking at him. "She's awake."

"Jennie?" Mom nearly dumped Nick on his rear in her effort to get to her daughter.

Dad lifted Nick into his arms and held him over the bed. "See, Daddy, I waked her up."

"Looks that way, son."

Mom pulled herself up and stroked Jennie's forehead. "Oh, honey. We were so worried. How are you feeling?"

"Um . . ." Her mouth was dry. "Need some water," she croaked.

Mom held the cup while Jennie sipped through a straw.

Jennie pushed away the cup and licked her lips. She looked from one to the other. *My family.* She still couldn't remember the details, but Jennie had no doubt that Nick was her brother and that Susan and Detective McGrady were her mom and dad.

"We've been waiting a long time for you to come back to us," Mom said. "I don't think I've ever prayed so hard in my life."

Nick reached for her.

"Careful, bud," Dad warned. "No hugs yet."

"Hi, Nick." Jennie smiled at him, reaching up to brush a finger against his soft cheek.

"See, I told ya she'd remember me."

"You'd be hard to forget."

Mom gave her a nod of approval.

Jennie's gaze drifted upward, latching on to her father's. "Do . . . do you know what happened to me? Why I was in the woods? Why someone. . . ?"

"The authorities are still gathering information. Why don't we talk about that later?"

When your mother and Nick aren't here, his expression seemed to say. He smiled. "The important thing is getting you well."

"Right, but . . ." Jennie wanted answers now. They were locked somewhere in her mind, but she needed help to release them. She hoped the police might be able to help.

Mom tightened her hold on Jennie's hand. "Are you remembering anything yet?"

"Not really." Jennie didn't mention the strange images and feelings that overcame her at times.

"The doctor says you'll probably regain your memory over time. And you used to write in your journal almost every day, so you can read those when we get you home. They should help."

"In the meantime," Dad said, "we'll help you reconstruct what you lost. As much as we know. You'll have a lot of help."

"Good." Jennie could think of nothing better than filling the black hole in her mind.

Dad set Nick on the foot of the bed and started for the door. "First we need to let the nurses know you're awake.

Dr. Mason wanted to be notified as soon as you regained consciousness."

Mom's eyes shone with happiness as she brushed Jennie's hair back from her face and tucked it behind her ears. "Welcome back."

Nick gently crawled up beside her and within a few minutes he'd fallen asleep snuggled against her. Mom started to take him, but Jennie didn't want to let him go. He belonged there. Maybe her mind didn't remember the little guy, but her heart sure did.

While they waited for Jennie's neurologist, her parents began filling her in on family details. Jennie enjoyed learning about the relatives, especially the complicated relationship between her mother and father and Aunt Kate and Uncle Kevin. And how she and her cousin Lisa had been best friends since early childhood. Mom showed her pictures from her wallet of various family members as she talked about them. Jennie loved hearing about her grandmother and immediately felt a connection.

"You take after the McGrady side of the family," Mom said. "Especially where law enforcement is concerned. You plan to study law. Unfortunately, you've already had your share of practical experiences."

"You mean about my helping the police solve crimes? Mr. Graham showed me an article in the paper."

"Maybe we shouldn't tell her about those, Jason." Mom tucked the photos back into her wallet. "I'd just as soon she not remember her knack for getting into trouble."

"Somehow I don't think that'll work. It's in her blood." He winked at her as if they shared a special secret.

"I want to know everything."

"Not right now." Dad lifted Nick off the bed. "We don't want to wear you out. Besides, Dr. Mason will be in soon. And I need to get back to work."

"Could you at least tell me about the dolphins?"

"Dolphins?" Mom and Dad asked together.

She told them about the dream she'd had in the ambulance on the way to the hospital.

"That would be your trip to Florida with your grand-mother." Dad chuckled. "Scott will be thrilled to hear about that. He and Ryan have been arguing about which one of them you'll remember first."

Jennie frowned. "Scott . . . he's the guy with green eyes?"

"Most likely."

"Scott and Ryan. Am I close to them?"

"Let's just say they're good friends," Dad answered quickly. "Ryan had to go back to school, but Scott's taken a week off from work and is staying with us."

"Are you sure he's just a friend?" Taking that much time sounded like more than friendship.

"You were supposed to meet Scott, Gavin, and Lisa at the Lewis River Falls trailhead on Saturday," Mom said. "He feels responsible for what happened to you. We all do."

"Susan, don't go there." Dad settled an arm around her shoulders. "We can't go back and change what happened. You had no idea she'd be abducted."

"Is that what happened?" Jennie asked. "When are we going to talk about it? When am I going to see Scott and Lisa . . . all of them?" Jennie asked, anxious for more information.

"Good morning." A white-haired man in a lab coat stepped into the room, ending their conversation.

"Jennie," her father said, "this is Dr. Mason."

Within two hours Jennie's eagerness to learn about her past melted into frustration. The neurologist and several students from the University Hospital found her case fascinating. Now that she was awake Dr. Mason had dozens of questions and tests to determine the extent of her memory loss and possible brain damage. He wanted to know everything she remembered and had her write down all the events from her first memory of waking up in the woods to the present.

Dr. Mason had a softspoken way about him, and while

he explained Jennie's condition to her, he was also teaching the medical students.

"Jennie, you appear to have what we call retrograde amnesia," he explained.

"I remember reading about that somewhere. Princess Diana's bodyguard had that."

"Right." He seemed impressed. "Do you recall any of the specifics?"

"His memory of the accident was lost, but he was still able to remember his family." Jennie frowned. "If I have that, how come I can't remember who I am or who my family is?"

"There are varying degrees of brain damage and memory loss. Your injury caused a loss of consciousness. The part of your brain that holds certain memories has apparently undergone some damage. Considering your other injuries and the fact that you've had a series of flashbacks, we suspect you may be suffering from post traumatic stress syndrome as well. Consequently, some of this memory loss may be emotional in its origin."

"Will I ever remember?"

"It's hard to tell at this point. Oftentimes the memory comes back in snatches. Some memories may be hidden for weeks or years. The good news is that you can reconstruct certain events. It may help you to write down your feelings and details from any flashbacks. You don't seem to have any cognitive impairment, and your motor skills are fine."

"Cognitive?"

"It appears that you are as intelligent now as you were before the accident. There are habits and personality traits—your faith, for example. You told me your first instinct was to pray."

Jennie smiled. "I remember praying while I was in the woods."

"Well, God certainly answered your prayers, Jennie. You are fortunate to be alive."

His words brought a sudden chill. Someone had wanted her dead. As far as she knew, that someone was still out there.

19

At lunchtime that day Lisa Calhoun bounced into the room. "Hi, Jennie. Your mom and dad said I could come in as long as I didn't wear you out."

The picture and her mother's description hadn't prepared Jennie for Lisa's bubbly personality. She wore her curly red hair wrapped in a knot at the top of her head with tendrils framing her roundish freckled face. She had green eyes that reminded her of the guy she'd seen in the dream. No, not a dream, a memory. Lisa reminded Jennie of Tigger in *Winnie the Pooh*.

Funny she'd remember something so inconsequential as a character in a book and not the names of the people she'd known all her life.

"You don't know me, either, do you?" Lisa's smile disappeared behind a look of concern.

"No."

"It's okay, you know. I mean—they told me you lost your memory, only I didn't quite believe you could ever forget me. We've been best friends forever. I probably know more about you than your parents do. Like who you hang out with. Your boyfriends, teachers, stuff like that. We tell each other everything . . . well, almost everything."

"Do I have many friends?"

"Tons." Lisa giggled.

"What's so funny?"

"Nothing." She sobered. "It just seems funny telling

you stuff that's already happened. Not funny . . . exactly."

"Definitely not funny." Jennie narrowed her eyes, assessing her cousin. "It's scary not knowing people."

"Why would it be scary?"

"Someone attacked me and left me in the woods to die. I don't know who did it. He could come in here any time, pretending to be a friend or a doctor or a lab tech, and I wouldn't recognize him. It could have been anyone. A man or a woman. Even you."

Lisa gasped. "Me! You don't really believe that, do you?"

Jennie shrugged. "How can I be sure?"

"Well, you have to trust somebody, and you might as well start with me." Lisa grinned, stuck her tongue out, and crossed her eyes. "Does this look like the face of a criminal?"

"Depends." Jennie felt the corners of her mouth shift into a smile. "You're right. I do have to trust someone."

"Mom says she can always tell if I'm telling the truth or not." Her gaze met Jennie's head on. "I would never lie to you, Jennie. Never. And I promise I'll stay with you all the time if you want. I know who you can trust and who you can't."

Do you? Are you sure? Jennie swallowed back the ever-present fear. *God, please let me remember. I hate not knowing who people are. And help me learn to trust my family and friends. Help me not to be so afraid.*

"I'm not sure I can handle having you around all the time." Then seeing she'd hurt Lisa's feelings, she added, "I'm sorry. It's just that you're so . . . hyper."

"It's okay. Mom says the same thing. I'll try not to talk quite so much." Lisa settled into the chair beside Jennie's bed and began tapping her bright yellow fingernails on the armrest. After several tedious moments she looked like a bubble ready to pop.

Taking pity on her, Jennie said, "Lisa, if you need to talk, talk. How about if I tell you when I need to rest?"

Lisa grinned and leaned forward. "I was just wondering

how it would feel to not remember anything. It would be awful to have to start all over again."

Jennie shook her head. "It's not like that. Not really. I know some things. It's like you wrote out this whold complicated essay and a bunch of it got erased. There are a lot of missing spaces."

"Which I'm supposed to help fill in." She leaned back and steepled her hands. "Let's see. We were talking about your friends, right?"

"Hmm." Jennie rubbed at a sore spot on her shoulder and turned onto her left side, facing Lisa.

"You actually have more guy friends than girls, I think. Not like real boyfriends—I mean, I know a lot of guys who would like to be, but you haven't been all that interested."

"Why?"

"Because for a long time you were totally wild about Ryan Johnson."

Jennie frowned, repeating the name. "Dad mentioned him. What's he like?"

"He's cute—blond, blue eyes, about two inches taller than you. He's nice. At least I used to think so before he started going out with Camilla. You were pretty steamed about that. He lives next door to Gram." Lisa pursed her lips. "We should go there. To the beach, I mean. I'll bet being there and staying with Gram would help you remember. The doctor says once you get into familiar surroundings you might."

"Have I been there a lot?"

"We go every chance we get. You love it there."

Jennie closed her eyes and tried to dredge up memories of the beach. She had no trouble visualizing an expanse of ocean, a sunset, fishing and sight-seeing boats dotting the horizon.

"What are you doing?"

"Visualizing. I'm picturing some rocks with the ocean below."

"There are rocks near Gram's house. You've been there

lots of times with Gram and me." She sighed. "You especially liked going with Ryan."

When Jennie tried to bring their faces into focus, the image slipped away.

"This is so cool. You're remembering."

"Not really. Tell me more about Ryan. Do I still like him?"

"As a friend. You told me he'd always be your friend."

"What about Scott?"

Lisa clasped her hands on her lap. "You two are kind of complicated. I think you really like Scott, but you also have a crush on Rocky. And then there's Dominic." She sighed, her face flushing. "He was so-o-o cute. Of course, he doesn't really count. I don't think he's been in touch with you since the cruise."

"I was on a cruise?"

"Gram and J.B. took us along on their honeymoon."

Jennie's head was starting to hurt again. Lisa had thrown out so many leads, she didn't know which one to follow.

"I'm confusing you, aren't I? I have a bad habit of going off in too many directions at once. I need to stick to the most important things." She chewed on her lower lip. "Let's see, I told you about Ryan. . . ."

"You mentioned that I had a crush on someone?"

"Rocky. He's a cop. Gorgeous blue eyes. He says you're a pain, but I think he secretly likes you. Only you're about six years younger than he is. Your dad would smash him if he even thought about asking you out." She smiled. "He sort of watches out for you. Like a big brother. Personally, I think maybe when you're out of college—well, he wouldn't be too old then. Of course, he has a girlfriend right now, but you never know."

Jennie frowned. "None of these guys sound too exciting."

"Actually, you aren't that serious about anyone, which is good. You're more interested in solving crimes and going to school. You're planning to go to law school. In fact, I have a theory about what happened to you."

"You do?" Jennie perked up. "What?"

"Well, you know how you're always investigating crimes. . . ?" She gave Jennie a sheepish look. "Oh well, I guess you wouldn't remember that, huh?"

"No, but I read about it in the paper. Did I really do all those things?"

"And more. Seems like everywhere you go, something weird happens."

"So what's your theory?"

"I think you went after the bank robbers." Lisa went on to tell her cousin about the bank robbery she'd witnessed. "See, on the radio Saturday morning there was an announcement telling people to be on the lookout for this gray Chevy. I'll bet you saw the car on your way up the mountain and followed them to their hideout and they caught you."

"Why would I do something so stupid—and dangerous? If I did see something like that, wouldn't I just call the police?"

"Maybe. But you don't carry a cell phone. And you have been known to get yourself into some scary situations."

Something about Lisa's comments struck a nerve, unsettling her in a way she couldn't explain. All she knew was that she didn't want to talk about her ordeal anymore. Her brain was a tangle of confusion and felt like it was closing down. Jennie lowered the head of her bed slightly and closed her eyes. Lisa had given her a lot to think about. Too much.

"Am I making you too tired?" Lisa asked. "Maybe I should go."

"Not yet. I need to ask you about something." She pushed all the information away and tried to refocus. There was one person she wanted to hear more about. "I think I remember Scott."

"You're kidding." Lisa shrugged. "Guess I don't blame you. He's really nice. And he thinks you're great. When you

didn't show up for the hike and we couldn't find you anywhere, he was so worried." She glanced at her watch.
"He'll be here in a few minutes. He and Ryan had a bet
about which one you'd remember first."

"You're kidding, right? They actually have a bet
going?"

"Stupid, huh?"

"Very." Jennie didn't know whether to laugh or be
angry. "Don't tell Scott about my remembering him. Anyway, I don't know for sure if it was him. Mom and Dad
seemed to think it was. All I know is the guy in my dream
had dark hair and green eyes, like yours."

"It's him. I know it is. He really likes you, Jen." Her eyes
shone with delight. "I won't say a word. By the way, a
bunch of the kids at school are talking about throwing you
a big party when you get well enough. We thought it would
be neat to have the party before you go back to school so
you can meet everyone. It'll be at Allison and B.J.'s house—
it's this huge mansion. You'll get to meet some of them
today after school." She began listing who would be there.

Meet them . . . how strange that seemed. Jennie didn't
bother asking about any of the friends Lisa mentioned.
She'd have to start taking notes so she could keep everyone
straight.

Lisa glanced at her watch again. "I have to get back to
school. I'm on my lunch break and got an excused absence
from my life skills class."

"Where do I go to school?"

"Trinity High—with me. It's a private Christian school.
Except you don't go full time. You're part homeschooled.
That's so you can take care of Nick. You're on the honor
roll and the swim team."

This piqued Jennie's interest. "Swim team? I'm a swim-
mer?"

"The best—well, maybe not *the* best, but DeeDee, your
coach, says if you really applied yourself, you could be an
Olympic contender."

"Hey, how's it going?" Scott stepped into the room carrying a bouquet of colorful flowers. His gaze skimmed over Lisa and collided with Jennie's.

Jennie felt her face flush, and as a mob of butterflies bounced off the walls of her stomach, she managed to say, "Good."

It is him. Her heart did another little flip. Jennie wanted to reach out and hug him but held herself in check.

He could be the enemy. He knew you'd be waiting.

But the dream wasn't frightening. It felt warm and peaceful. He was with the dolphins. He can be trusted. He couldn't have hurt you. He was with Lisa and Gavin, Jennie argued against her fears.

They could be in on it together. What if they. . . ?

No, don't even think it. These are your friends. You have to stop being so suspicious.

"Um . . . I brought these for you," Scott said, "but looks like you've got plenty."

"Thanks. They're nice." Jennie breathed in the scent of the carnations and scanned the room looking for an empty space. She'd noticed the dozen or so bouquets of flowers and get-well balloons earlier, but she had no idea who had brought them. She'd have to look at the cards later. "Put them here." She moved the bedside table.

After setting down the flowers he stood at the foot of the bed, his gaze lingering on her face but not quite meeting her eyes. "You look better."

"Than what?" She offered him a smile, appreciating his efforts to lift her spirits.

"The other guy?"

Jennie winced. Her stomach cramped into a tight ball.

"I mean . . . you wouldn't have given up without a fight. I should know."

Her stomach knotted up with fear at his innocent comment. Tears pooled in her eyes and dripped back into her hair before she could reach for the tissue.

"I'm sorry."

"Not your fault." Jennie sniffed. There was a long pause as she blew her nose and pulled herself together.

Scott looked like he'd rather be feeding sharks than stay in the same room with her. She wanted to explain her strange emotional response but didn't know how.

"It's not you," Lisa told Scott. "We never know when she's going to cry or have one of her flashbacks." Lisa gave Jennie a conspiratorial look. "Oh, I guess I really should introduce you. Jennie—" Lisa went to stand beside him— "this is Scott Chambers."

"I know." Jennie sniffed and drew in a deep breath.

Lisa frowned. "I thought you weren't going to tell him."

"I changed my mind."

Scott looked from one to the other. "What's going on? What weren't you going to tell me?"

"That Jennie remembers you. In fact, you're the only person she does remember."

"Really?" Scott flashed her a wide smile.

"The first human." She told him about the dolphins and palm trees she'd dreamed about during the ambulance ride into town.

He nodded. "Dolphin Island. We had a great time . . . when I wasn't getting into trouble. You saved my life, Jennie."

"I did?"

Lisa hitched herself on the end of the bed, pride filling her eyes. "She does that a lot—saving people."

Jennie didn't respond and Scott just nodded.

"I have to go," Lisa said suddenly. She gave Jennie a hug, said good-bye to Scott, and promised to see her after school.

Jennie asked her to bring her some paper to make notes on. With all the people she'd heard about, she was going to need some way of keeping track. Lisa agreed and Jennie turned back to Scott. "Tell me about Dolphin Island."

Scott spent the next half hour filling her in on the most incredible story of how Jennie had solved a two-year-old murder. Jennie hoped Scott would trigger something, make her remember more details in that chapter of her life, but nothing more came.

After a few minutes Jennie could hardly keep her eyes open and apologized as Scott's face became a blur. She let her eyes drift closed.

———

An hour later when she awoke, Scott was gone. Another guy had taken his place in the chair beside her bed. The blond hair and blue eyes and the way her heart tripped over itself when he smiled told her it could only be one person.

"Hi." Jennie raised a hand and let it drop back onto the bed. "You must be Rocky."

"Hey." He stuffed the small note pad he'd been writing on into the front left pocket of his denim shirt. "Are you regaining your memory or was that a lucky guess?"

"Lisa told me about you."

"Ah." He leaned back in the chair and rubbed his clean-shaven chin.

"She told me you were a police officer." Jennie frowned. "But you're not wearing a uniform."

"I'm on leave. Took a bullet in the back a few weeks ago."

Jennie winced. "And you're up walking around?"

"Had a good doctor who put me in rehab right away. Fortunately, I bounced back pretty quickly. *Un*fortunately, the chief won't let me come back to work for another two weeks." He leaned forward, putting his elbows on his knees. "I didn't come here to talk about my problems. Came by to see how *you* were doing."

"I'd be a lot better if my memory would come back."

"Would it help to know the authorities are making some progress?"

"Yeah. What?" Jennie sat up straighter and clasped her hands around her knees.

"Has anyone told you about the bank robbery you witnessed last Friday?"

Jennie frowned. "Lisa told me about it. I actually witnessed one? That must have been pretty scary."

"I'm sure it was, even for you. That's one of the reasons

131

I came by. Your dad asked me to talk to you. Let you know what we've got so far. He's hoping it might trigger your memory."

"Why didn't Dad come?"

"He's tied up on a double homicide. I bumped into him earlier and told him I was thiking of paying you a visit."

"So what did you find out?"

"Well, for starters, they found your car."

"Great!" Jennie grinned, then sobered at his dour expression. "That's good, right?"

"Yes, but it poses some problems."

"What do you mean?"

"The police here in Portland and in Vancouver have been working closely with the Clark County Sheriff's Department and the Forestry Service on your case. The investigating offcers found your car near the Grahams' cabin. It had been hidden in some blackberry thickets."

"Um . . . I guess that means I drove to the cabin."

"Looks that way, since your prints are the only ones on the steering wheel. They're still trying to piece it all together, but from the evidence they've found it looks like there's a connection between your disappearance and the bank robberies."

Since her cousin had come up with a connection as well, Jennie wondered if she really had gone after the bank robbers. Hungry for details, she urged him to go on.

"You had a passenger. Whoever it was put a bullethole through the driver's-side door."

Jennie shuddered and touched the bandage on her thigh. "Is that how my leg got hurt?"

"No. They figure that happened in the woods."

"How can they tell?"

"They found signs of a struggle and blood evidence where the Graham girls found you, but there was no blood in the car. My guess is that one of the bank robbers needed a car and yours was available. Knowing you, you objected and tried to escape. He fired his weapon, probably to scare you."

Jennie felt the blood drain from her face and pinched her eyes shut to ward off another flashback. She covered her ears to block the deafening explosion of gunfire. The image passed quickly, leaving only a blur of color and utter silence.

"Are you okay?" Rocky was on his feet, leaning over the railing.

She hauled in a deep breath and released it slowly. "I get these . . . flashbacks." She told him about those she'd had so far.

"If you can, you might want to write down the details, Jennie. Hopefully you'll be able to come up with an accurate description of these guys. Right now you're about the only person in a position to identify them."

Suddenly Jennie wasn't sure she wanted her memory back—wasn't sure she wanted to remember her abductors or anything about them. *When they realize you're still alive and could identify them, they'll come after you again.*

20

"It might be a while before I remember." Jennie tried to put her fears to rest.

"I hope not." Rocky sat back in his chair.

"You said the police found some evidence linking what happened to me to these bank robberies? Finding my car and knowing I was abducted doesn't necessarily mean it was the bank robbers, does it?" As much as she hated thinking about her ordeal, she had to know what the police had found and how she'd become involved.

"We found some prints on your car that match a set the Vancouver police lifted from a car that was abandoned near Vancouver Mall. They have witnesses who say it was one of the getaway cars. Also, we've been able to link a string of stolen and abandoned cars to this ring of bank robberies."

"Then I don't need to remember, right? Won't the prints tell you who did it? And you said there were other witnesses."

"So far we haven't been able to come up with a match on the prints. We're still working on that. As for witnesses, the guys were always in disguise."

"What if I don't remember?"

"Oh, I have no doubt we'll get them eventually. But we want them now, before . . ." He hesitated. His concerned gaze met Jennie's eyes, and she knew.

"Before they come after me?"

"That is a concern. Your dad wants around-the-clock guards put on you, but we just don't have enough officers or time for that. But don't worry. We have it covered. I've offered to keep an eye on you when your dad isn't around. Your grandmother and J.B. will help as well. I guess they're here for a few days to help out."

"That's really nice of you."

He shrugged. "Not really. We're just covering the bases."

Knowing she'd have around-the-clock guards lessened her fears. Still, she wouldn't be able to rest until the criminals were caught and in prison. "I just don't understand why you haven't been able to catch them yet."

"They're resourceful. In each case they leave so many rabbit trails it's almost impossible to follow up on the leads. Finding their hideout was a big break for us. If the Graham girls hadn't found you, we'd still be going in circles."

Jennie touched the still-tender lump on the back of her head. "I'm sure glad Corisa and Brandy showed up when they did."

Rocky's sincere blue gaze met hers. "So am I."

He cleared his throat and went on. "Besides the bullet hole and prints, we found a couple twenty-dollar bills in the trunk. The serial numbers match those taken in Friday's robbery."

"Have there been any more robberies?"

"There were two last Saturday up north. Nothing since. We're thinking they either left the area or are waiting for things to cool down." Rocky looked pensive.

"You don't think I had anything to do with the robberies, do you? I mean . . . it couldn't have been me. I was at the falls waiting for . . ." Jennie swallowed back a newly formed lump.

A woman in a lab coat paused at the door to Jennie's room. Her gaze drifted from Rocky to Jennie. She took a couple of steps inside and stopped.

"Did you need something?" Rocky asked.

The woman came closer. "Hi, Jennie. I . . . um . . . I'm

Julie Larson." She pointed to her name badge. "I was working in the ER when Jennie was brought in. Thought I'd stop and see how things are going." She smiled. "You certainly look better."

"Thanks, I think." Jennie didn't remember seeing her in the ER, but her memory wasn't exactly reliable. Julie had straight blond hair cut in a shag that framed her thin face. She was in her forties. There was a toughness about her that Jennie found unsettling.

You find everything unsettling, she reminded herself.

"No problem. I like to follow up on my patients."

She smoked, Jennie realized as Julie neared the bed. That disturbed her even more than the toughness, but she wasn't sure why. The scent wasn't overpowering, just present as it was in several of the hospital staff who'd cared for her. In fact, Julie had apparently tried to hide the smell with a mint. *You have to stop being so suspicious.*

"I heard you were regaining your memory," Julie said.

"Some."

"That's great. Your nurse says there's a good chance you'll regain all of it."

"I hope so."

Julie glanced at Rocky. "I'll bet you're anxious for her memory to return since she can identify the bank robbers?"

He raised an eyebrow and eyed her suspiciously. "How did you know about the connection?"

"Heard it this morning on my way to work. The sheriff's department finally gave in to the press and held a news conference. Pretty disturbing. Did you know Jennie's considered a suspect?"

"The sheriff said that?" Rocky asked.

"Not exactly. The reporter did. Apparently some woman called in to the news station with an anonymous tip. They recorded her and played it on the air. The witness said she'd seen a red Mustang at her bank during the robbery and thought it might have been used as a getaway car." Julie looked back at Jennie. "She described you as the driver."

"Jennie was at the bank that got hit last Friday," Rocky informed her. "She'd gone in to make a deposit."

"Oh, it wasn't that bank. It was the one up in Woodland on Saturday."

"Has to be a prank call!" Rocky ran a hand through his sandy hair. "That's ridiculous."

"I couldn't agree with you more. Just thought you might like to know." Julie tipped her head, offering Jennie a sympathetic look. "I'm sure once you regain your memory, you'll be able to set matters right."

Rocky left later that afternoon when her father arrived. Since the visit with Julie, she'd been stewing about her possible involvement in the holdups. Though Rocky tried to tell her the witness was mistaken and that there were a lot of red Mustangs out there, the insinuation that she might have been one of the bank robbers haunted her.

What kind of life did I lead before? Was I leading a double life? Could she trust those who told her she was innocent of wrongdoing?

"What if I am one of the bank robbers?" Jennie asked Dad.

"You are not!" her father said emphatically. His mood sullen, he'd listened to her relate her earlier conversation with the ER nurse and Rocky. The woman was wrong. There is no way you would take part in a bank robbery."

"Are you sure I didn't do it?"

"Jennie, how would you feel if I agreed and told you that you actually *were* capable of such a thing?"

"Terrible, I guess."

"Right now if I told you to go rob a bank, would you do it?"

She scrunched up her face. "Of course not."

"See? You wouldn't because you are not now, nor have you ever been, a criminal."

"The doctor said that after a head injury a person's personality can change."

Dad placed his hand over hers. "Princess, look at me."

She met his gaze, then looked away. She wanted more than anything to believe him. But how could he know for sure? Even the sheriff doubted her. He'd come in while Rocky was there. "The sheriff asked me all kinds of questions and acted like he didn't believe me. He said I'd previously been arrested for possession."

Dad covered his eyes and rubbed his forehead.

"It's true, isn't it?"

"The drugs were planted in your car. You were completely innocent, and those charges were dropped. You don't have a criminal record."

"Are you sure, Dad? Are you absolutely sure?"

"Yes," he said reassuringly. "We don't have all the answers yet. The sheriff's department has search teams out there now combing a five-mile radius around the campground where you were supposed to meet Lisa. They're hoping to find the car your abductor left behind. Like I said, I don't know exactly what happened. But I do know this, princess. You were a victim. I looked over the place myself. They kept you locked up in a closet. You were beaten and taken into the woods. . . ."

A scene flashed in Jennie's head. Terror shot through her like a bolt of lightning.

Her dad was on his feet and at her side in an instant. "What happened? Are you in pain?"

She gasped for air and gripped his arm. "Another flashback. I saw him, Dad. I saw his face."

21

"Take it easy, honey." Dad's arms went around her, stroking her hair. "You're safe now. We're not going to let anything happen to you."

She wrapped her arms around his neck, her tears soaking into his shirt. "I want to go home. Please."

"I don't know about that, but we'll call Dr. Mason and see what he says."

An hour later Dr. Mason stood at her bedside listening to her arguments for going home.

"I'll be more comfortable. My grandmother is there to help with cleaning and stuff so I won't get too tired."

"I agree."

"And being home might help me remember faster and—" She paused when his words finally sank in. "Oh. So I can go home?"

Dr. Mason grinned. "As you said, you'll be more comfortable there. *But* I still need to keep you under observation." Looking at her father he added, "Bring her to the office the day after tomorrow. Sooner if there's a problem or you notice any significant changes. I'll have my nurse call you and let you know what time. Jennie"—he leveled a skeptical gaze at her—"are you sure you want to go?"

"Positive."

"I'm concerned about the way these flashbacks are affecting you emotionally. Besides the head injury, you've apparently been through severe trauma. I'm—"

"I can handle it," Jennie said quickly, fearing he'd change his mind.

He pursed his lips. "Possibly. The thing is, Jennie, I suspect you're a very independent young lady."

Dad nodded in agreement. "And stubborn."

"Good. Jennie, your parents have told me about your propensity for solving crimes. And I can certainly understand if you feel the need to solve the mystery surrounding your injuries. But your job is to rest and relax. Don't try so hard to remember. The part of your brain that seems to be responsible for memory has been seriously injured. The only thing I want you to work on is taking it easy and letting your body heal."

"That means no detective work," Dad insisted.

Jennie bit her lip. "I hardly think I'm in any condition to do anything like that."

Dad gave her a why-don't-I-believe-you look but didn't comment.

Dr. Mason opened Jennie's chart and jotted something down. "I don't want Jennie to be alone. If her memory does return, it could be rather traumatic for her."

"You don't have to worry about that," Dad assured him. "Part of Jennie's fear and mine is that whoever abducted and beat her may come back to finish the job. I'll arrange to have someone with her at all times."

"Okay, then." Dr. Mason flashed her a smile. "You can leave as soon as you're ready. I'm going to give you a prescription for those headaches." He went on to restate the discharge instructions as he wrote them down.

As he talked and wrote, Jennie could feel the anxiety rise from the pit of her stomach and move into her neck and shoulders. A lump settled in her throat. Was she doing the right thing? *Of course you are.* But somehow Jennie wasn't so sure.

Within thirty minutes Dad picked her up in front of the hospital. Once they reached the freeway Jennie leaned back against the seat and tried to relax. *It's going to be all right,* she told herself for the umpteenth time.

Jennie stared out the window of her parents' Oldsmobile. Her anxiety gradually subsided. In its place came a strong sense of determination. True, she wanted to go home for all the reasons she'd told her father and Dr. Mason. But she had another reason as well. Jennie wanted to find out all she could about the bank robbers. Being in the hospital had made her feel vulnerable. Any one of the dozens of people she came in contact with each day could be a killer. The ER staff, the doctors, the IV nurses . . . even the housekeepers.

Two different housekeepers had been in that day. One, a Russian woman named Lana, had been friendly and cheerful. She could hardly speak English and had rattled on about how her sister would be coming from Russia to spend Thanksgiving and Christmas with her. She kept slipping from broken English into Russian, and Jennie kept having to remind her that she didn't understand.

She'd felt comfortable with Lana. The other housekeeper, however, had made her uneasy. He hadn't spoken, and she'd been unable to read his name tag. He'd washed the floor, and several times Jennie had looked up from the book she'd been reading and caught him watching her. He never made eye contact. There was something about him. . . .

There's something weird about almost everyone you see, she reminded herself. He was probably just shy. As she thought about it, he did seem kind of cute. Maybe he'd just been flirting with her. *Right.* With her black eyes and bruises she looked about as attractive as a toad. Of course, he might have just been curious.

Jennie sighed. She was tired of being on edge, tired of suspecting nearly everyone she saw. Somehow she had to remember her abductors so the police could catch them and put them behind bars. And despite what Dr. Mason and her father had told her, Jennie planned to help.

She hoped the information she gleaned from the newspapers and from talking to people would help her remember. Everyone had talked about her detecting skills.

Though she wasn't completely certain what being a sleuth involved, maybe it was about time she started acting like one.

One of the first things she planned to do was drive into the mountains and up to the Grahams' cabin. She'd had several flashbacks there. Jennie gulped to dispel another wave of fear. Maybe she'd even sit in the closet for a while. If being there didn't bring back her memory, nothing would. Well, that wasn't quite true. Dr. Mason had said her brain would need time to heal. Still, driving up to the cabin wouldn't hurt.

Jennie shifted in her seat. "Dad, what happened to my car? Rocky said the deputies found it."

"It's been impounded." He glanced at her and smiled. "Don't worry, you'll get it back eventually. I'm not sure whether or not your insurance will cover bullet holes. Your mom's checking on it. Don't worry," he added before Jennie could protest. "We'll have it repaired one way or another. It'll need a new paint job as well, since the sides are all scratched up."

"So when can I have it back?"

"Soon enough. You won't be driving for a while anyway."

Jennie rubbed her forehead. "I know the doctor said I should rest, but he didn't say I couldn't go for a drive."

Dad shook his head. "Let's not split hairs, okay?"

"I want to go back to the cabin."

"I know. And I'll take you."

"Today?"

"Jennie, it's late."

"Tomorrow, then."

"Might be too soon."

"Dr. Mason said I should go back to where it happened."

"Eventually, but not yet."

Jennie pulled her loosened hair back and redid her ponytail. "I need to go, Dad. I can't explain it, but I just have to."

He gave her an exasperated look. "I'll talk to your mother, and we'll see what Dr. Mason says. Though I'm not sure when we can make the trip."

"Lisa can drive me. Or one of my . . . my friends."

"No." He gave her a sharp look. "Jennie, you are not to go up there alone or with one of your friends."

"Do you think the bank robbers are still around there?"

"I doubt it. The sheriff's department has been keeping a close eye on the area."

"So it's safe."

"Relatively, but there's always a chance."

"Maybe Mom could—"

"Absolutely not. She's in no condition to drive that far. She's supposed to be resting."

His concerned look drove thoughts of the mountain cabin from her mind. "Is something wrong with her? I mean, I know she's pregnant."

"There are some complications." Dad's jaw tightened. "The doctor is very concerned. With all the activity over the last few days . . ."

"You mean staying at the hospital with me?"

"Partly. I tried to get her to stay home more, but she wouldn't hear of it. Said she'd be worse off at home worrying than sitting with you. She's been trying to do too much around the house." He went on to explain Mom's condition. "I don't want you to worry. You need to concentrate on getting well."

"But who's going to help with cleaning and making meals and taking care of Nick?"

"Gram has been coming in every day, and Kate's helping when she can." Glancing back to check for traffic, he moved into the right lane to take the next exit. "We're almost home. Do you recognize anything?"

Jennie looked around for familiar landmarks. She may as well have been traveling in a foreign country. "No."

"Well, maybe being home will help."

"I hope so."

Minutes later they pulled into the driveway. Jennie

eased herself out of the car, closed the door, and leaned on it for support.

"Hang on a sec, princess, I'll give you a hand."

"Jennie, Jennie!" Nick bounced down the stairs and cannonballed toward them. "You're home."

"Whoa." Dad raced around the car and swooped Nick up before he could collide with Jennie. "Take it easy, son. Your sister's not all that steady on her feet yet."

That was an understatement. At the hospital they'd taken her to the car in a wheelchair. Now she faced the prospect of walking into the house on legs that suddenly felt like rubber. After hugging her insistent brother, Jennie looked up at the two-story Victorian. "Neat house," she said.

"Glad you like it." Dad hugged her to him. "Welcome home, princess." He set Nick down. "How about opening the door for us, Nick?"

"Sure." He ran ahead. "You gonna carry Jennie like you did me when I was sick?"

Dad chuckled. "Only if she wants me to."

"I can make it. I just need to hold on to your arm." She got as far as the steps when her knees buckled.

"Up you go." Ignoring her protests, Dad lifted her into his arms and carried her the rest of the way in. Once inside, he strode across the tiled entry and deposited her on the living room couch.

Mom maneuvered her body out of the recliner she'd been resting in and gave Jennie a hug. "I'm so glad you're home. We've missed you so much."

Like a flock of sea gulls hoping for a handout, Jennie's family gathered around her. Nick dropped to the floor near her head with a book. "Mama said I could read to you."

"You can, honey." Mom brushed Jennie's hair back and kissed her forehead. "But at least let her get out of her jacket."

Dad eased the jacket off her shoulders. "Where are Mom and J.B.?"

"Shopping. When Gram heard our girl was coming

home she insisted on making Jennie's favorite dinner."

"What's my favorite dinner?"

Mom grinned. "We'll let it be a surprise."

Coming home both excited and tired Jennie. She leaned her head against the couch and felt herself drifting off.

"Looks like you could use a nap," Mom said. "Honey, why don't you take her upstairs? Her bed will be much more comfortable."

Jennie was so tired she didn't protest and let him carry her up the stairs.

Dad set her down on the bed and told her to sleep tight.

"I will," she said to the closing door. And she would—soon. Seeing her room perked her up. She looked around, hopeful at first, then disappointed when nothing jarred her memory. "Don't give up," she murmured. She needed to be patient. *"Relax,"* Dr. Mason had said. *"Don't try so hard."*

Jennie leaned back against her pillows and tried following her doctor's orders. She liked her room. It had a peaceful quality about it. In keeping with the Victorian style of the house, the bed had a white metal frame and an ivory comforter. Not a lot of frills and lace, but just enough. The computer perched on a student desk somehow seemed out of place. Later, when she felt more alert, she'd turn it on and delve into its secrets.

She closed her eyes and several minutes later opened them again. As tired as she felt, she couldn't stop thinking and wondering. A person's room told a lot about their personality. She wanted to know more about herself. Find herself.

One thing was clear—Jennie liked stuffed animals. There had to be at least a dozen scattered around the room. Most of them sat on the seat tucked in a large window.

Jennie thought about getting up and going back downstairs, but she wasn't certain she could face her family again so soon. Instead, she went to her closet and stood in front of the full-length mirror. She was thin. And pale. Her dark blue eyes had a haunted look. Her face was still bruised, looking like someone had painted it in a wash of purple, brown, and yellow. She pushed her hair away from her face and ran her fingers through it. In pictures she'd seen of herself, she'd often worn it in a ponytail or a braid. Picking up a brush, she raked through the tangles. Several minutes later she secured the braid with a hair band.

Maybe if she put on some makeup. Jennie rooted around in the dresser drawers, then made her way to the bathroom. There wasn't much—an old bottle of foundation and a tube of mascara. *Guess you don't wear much of it.* Jennie dabbed on some foundation, thinking to hide some of the bruising, then washed it off again. It hurt too much to rub her face, especially the bruise along her jaw.

How could she not remember someone hurting her like that? *How can you not remember yourself or your family?* Jennie squeezed her eyes shut as another flashback hit. This time she saw herself lying on the ground. Dead. In an instant it was gone, leaving her shaken to the core.

Why would I think I was dead? I didn't die, did I, Lord? She leaned over, resting her head in her hands, elbows on the counter. *Is this some kind of crazy dream? Am I going to wake up and realize that none of this has happened?*

Jennie raised her head. She didn't understand the flashback. She wasn't dead. Whatever had happened was real. *I'm here and I'm alive, and my name is Jennie McGrady.* The stranger in the mirror just looked at her.

———

When Jennie awoke, the digital clock on the bedside stand read 6:30 P.M. After her explorations, Jennie had been more than ready for her nap. She'd fallen asleep immediately and been out for over an hour.

Delicious smells from the kitchen made her stomach growl. She should go downstairs, but she wasn't certain she wanted to just yet. In the short time she'd been there, her room had become a safe haven. A streetlight spread its golden glow across the front yard and into her bedroom window. It drew Jennie like a beacon. She stroked the cushions on the window seat and moved aside a menagerie of stuffed animals.

Holding a cuddly brown teddy bear, she sat on the seat and looked out into the yard and down the street. She'd lived here all her life, her parents had said. And Jennie didn't doubt it. Her room, the view, the window seat, all had a comfortable, almost familiar feel to them. Of course, it could just be that she'd spent the last two hours there.

Jennie squeezed the soft, squishy bear against her chest. This was her space, her home, her family. She belonged here, yet part of her felt like an intruder.

Will I ever get my memory back?

Jennie leaned her head against a pillow. She liked the neighborhood. It was old and established. Her gaze drifted from one house to another, eventually landing on a car that slowed down and stopped in front of a neighbor's house just beyond the reaches of the streetlight. The driver cut the lights, but no one got out. For several minutes she watched and waited.

Jennie saw a flash of orange as the occupant pulled out a cigarette lighter and lit a cigarette. Her heart shifted into high gear. A chill shuddered through her. For an instant the light illuminated a fraction of the driver's face, giving it a ghoulish appearance. Then it was gone. Jennie stared at the smoke drifting out of the car and the hand sticking out of the window holding a cigarette.

Panic shrieked through her. *They've come back. They know where you live!*

22

Jennie jumped up and fumbled with the blinds. When she finally got them lowered and closed, she collapsed back on the seat.

"What's wrong with me?" She clutched at the cushions and pushed herself up. "I have to stop being so scared."

Leaning over, she lifted a slat in the blinds and looked out. The car was still there. It was a white newer model, but she couldn't tell the make or read the license plate. She hadn't seen it in the neighborhood before. "Oh, that's rich," she muttered. "You can't remember *ever* seeing the neighborhood before, so what makes you think you'd remember a car?"

Disgusted with herself, she moved away from the window, hating the way these random thoughts seemed intent on stirring her up inside when she least expected it. There were other cars parked in the street, but none of them made her react so . . . so . . . Jennie searched for a word to explain. *Desperate. Terrified.* Why that car?

It's nothing, she tried to tell herself again. *Probably someone waiting for a friend to come out. A guy waiting for his date. Or a smoker needing a fix before going inside.* It could have been any number of things. If she felt stronger she'd simply go out and ask. But somehow the thought of confronting the person in the car made her skin crawl.

Running a hand through her hair, Jennie made her way to the light switch near the door. She had almost reached it when she heard a click. Her heart leaped to her throat.

The bedroom door opened, letting in a wide patch of light from the hallway. A tall, lanky woman with salt-and-pepper hair stepped in.

"Jennie? It's Gram. . . ."

Jennie sank back against the wall and let out the breath she'd been holding. It was just her grandmother.

"Oh, there you are. Why are you wandering around in the dark?"

"I . . . I was just going to turn the light on."

"Well, no need. Dinner's about ready. Thought we'd better wake you." She stretched out her arms in greeting.

Jennie moved into them, releasing her fears. She could almost feel herself melting into the warmth and comfort she found there. *You're safe*, a voice from deep inside seemed to say. She worried about the abrupt change in moods.

"My goodness, child." Gram put her at arm's length and frowned. "What's wrong? You look so pale, and you're shaking."

"Had a scare." Jennie released a shaky laugh. "There was a car parked on the other side of the street, and I thought for a minute they might be watching . . ." Feeling embarrassed, Jennie shook her head. "It's nothing. Since the, um . . . since I woke up in the woods, I've been scared of nearly everything and everyone. It was probably one of the neighbors or . . ."

Gram shushed her. "After what's happened you have every reason to be concerned. Let's have a look." Gram closed the door, plunging the room back into darkness. Taking Jennie's hand, she quickly moved toward the window and looked outside.

"Hmm. I don't see anything unusual. Can you point it out to me?"

"Sure, it's . . ." Jennie frowned. "It's gone."

"Tell me what you saw." With an arm around Jennie's shoulders, Gram guided her back to the door and into the hall.

Holding the banister with one hand and Gram's arm with the other, Jennie descended the stairs and reluctantly explained what she'd seen. "I feel silly."

"No reason to," Gram insisted. "What you feel is as important as what you see. Sometimes more so. You have always had a highly tuned intuition. I suspect it's a McGrady trait since you and I and your father seem to be blessed with it. You haven't always listened to your intuition, but then, neither have I."

"So you think I might be right?" The thought both comforted and unsettled her.

"Perhaps. My experience has been that it usually pays to heed your intuitive reaction to a situation. It's almost like a built-in warning system that God gives us as protection."

"I think mine has been short-circuited."

"Understandable. Still, I'd like you to let us know the moment your instincts tell you something is wrong so we can at least check it out."

"I'm not sure that's such a good idea." Jennie paused at the bottom of the stairs. Her legs had turned to mush again, but she was determined to make it to the table.

"Why ever not?" Gram seemed to sense Jennie's difficulty and held her more firmly.

"You'd be spending all your time checking out people."

"Well, you let us worry about that. The important thing is that you let us know when you're feeling uneasy about someone—anyone."

The conversation ended abruptly as Gram settled Jennie into a chair at the head of the beautifully decorated table. "Wow!" Jennie's gaze took in the ivory lace tablecloth, the elegant fall centerpiece, and the spread of sparkling china, silver, and crystal.

Nick tore out of the kitchen and headed straight for Jennie.

"Nick!" His father issued a stern warning.

Nick stopped just short of her. She reached out and hugged him.

"Dad and me setted the table special for you." He gazed up at her, his blue eyes wide with excitement.

"It looks like you're expecting royalty."

"We are, princess." Dad came in carrying a huge oval platter of one very large fish. "You." He set the platter down in the center of the table.

Mom came in behind him, squeezed Jennie's hand, planted a kiss on her forehead, then pulled out the chair next to her. "We wanted your first evening home to be really special."

"Who all's coming?" Jennie counted eight place settings.

"Just us. Gram, J.B., me, your dad, Nick, Scott, and Lisa. I sent Scott to pick her up. They should be here any minute."

As if on cue the front door opened. Laughter filled the entry. Lisa's cheeks were flushed from the cool night air. She whipped off her dark green headband, dropped a duffel bag on the floor of the closet, and shrugged out of her iridescent green jacket. Jennie found herself relaxing even more at her cousin's easy manner and the joy that seemed to follow her around like an aura.

Lisa could have been a model. She was that gorgeous. Under her heavy coat she'd worn jeans and a soft, cotton candy pink sweater. Watching Scott and Lisa together stirred something inside her. They made a cute couple. She had no idea why the thought came to mind or why—if Scott was supposed to be Jennie's boyfriend—she felt no jealousy or animosity at the idea.

Scott, however, didn't seem to notice how cute Lisa was. As he shed his coat, his gaze captured Jennie's. "Hey, I was beginning to think you were avoiding me."

"Why would you think that?" Jennie returned his smile.

Dad chuckled. "Scott came back to the hospital just after you checked out."

"Yeah, and by the time I got back here, you were taking a nap."

Before Jennie could respond, Gram and J.B. came in carrying the rest of the meal. Once they were all seated, her father asked the blessing and made a point of praying especially for Jennie's health and safety.

By the time they'd finished dinner, Jennie had no trouble believing that this was her favorite meal. When she wasn't eating the delicious fresh grilled salmon, wild rice, roasted veggies, and sourdough bread, she was laughing at the stories each person at the table told about his or her most memorable times spent together with Jennie.

After the meal Lisa pulled out the Scrabble game and insisted Jennie and Scott play with her. Not wanting to leave Nick out, Jennie asked him to be her partner. She only lasted through half a dozen plays before admitting defeat. "Hate to do this, guys, but I can hardly keep my eyes open."

Scott looked disappointed but didn't say anything.

"No, not yet," Lisa pouted. "I'm ahead of you for the first time in ages. You can't quit now."

"Are you saying I usually beat you?" Jennie asked.

"Not usually. All the time." She grinned. "But I slaughter you in Monopoly so it's a fair trade."

Jennie rubbed the back of her neck. "I'd really like to stay up, but I'm totaled."

"I guess I can understand that." Lisa eyed the scores and turned to Scott. "Want to finish the game with me?"

"I do," Nick piped up. "I bet I can beat you."

Lisa rubbed his hair. "No way."

"Yes, I can. I can spell all kinds of stuff."

"No more games for you, young man." Mom came in from the kitchen, where the four adults had been drinking coffee and tea. "We're going to have some ice cream and baked apples, and then you have to go to bed."

"Ice cream!" Nick popped up, jumped over Jennie's legs, and hustled into the kitchen.

"He doesn't like ice cream by any chance, does he?" Scott dumped his tiles on the board.

"Not at all," Mom teased. "What ever gave you that idea? Would you all like some?"

"Not me." Jennie started putting letters into the bag. "I'm going to bed."

Lisa chewed on her lower lip. "I guess I'll skip it too. Oh, I almost forgot. Is it okay if I spend the night? I brought my stuff just in case."

"I suppose." Mom glanced at Jennie. "Are you up to that?"

Not wanting to hurt Lisa's feelings, she agreed.

"Great. I guess I should have talked to you first, but we always . . . I mean, we always used to stay over at each other's houses."

"It's okay. Just don't expect me to stay up and talk."

"I won't."

Somehow Jennie didn't quite believe her.

One thing Jennie especially liked about her family was the affection they showed to one another. It seemed like they were always touching or hugging or kissing her. Tonight was no exception. As Jennie and Lisa headed for the stairs, the entire family gathered around them.

Nick, with ice cream already smeared on his face, ran in, gave her his superduper bear hug, got sticky ice cream on her cheek, then ran back to finish his dessert.

"Good night, sweetheart." Mom gave her an especially long hug, telling her for the tenth time how great it was to have her home again.

Dad wanted to know if she wanted him to carry her upstairs.

She kissed his cheek. "I'll yell if I can't make it."

Gram held her close. "We haven't talked much about your memory loss tonight, darling, but I want you to know we love you and we're all here for you. We'll help you get through this no matter how long it takes. I promise."

Jennie knew they'd help her as much as they could. But would it be enough?

"That goes for me, as well, luv." J.B. hugged her to him. "Sweet dreams."

They repeated their good-nights to Lisa and filed back into the kitchen. Scott stood in the entry with them, looking uncomfortable. "Guess I'd better say good-night too. Um . . . that dessert sounds pretty good."

"Scott, I . . ." Jennie paused. "I'm sorry. I wish I felt more like visiting, but—"

"Hey, don't worry about it. I'll be around for another

day or two. We'll have lots of time."

"Right. Thanks for understanding. And for staying. That means a lot."

He paused, looking like he was about to kiss her. She hoped he wouldn't.

"No problem." He lifted his arm in a halfhearted wave and headed toward the kitchen.

Jennie sighed and turned toward Lisa. Before she could say anything, Lisa shrugged. "Don't worry about him. He'll have fun talking to the others. Knowing Nick, he'll get Scott to read a bunch of bedtime stories to him."

Remembering what Nick had said in the hospital, Jennie said, "I thought that was my job."

"Not tonight. Your job is to hang out with me. I still have a lot to tell you."

They started up the stairs, with Jennie leaning heavily against the banister. "I thought we weren't going to stay up and talk."

Lisa flashed her an impish grin. "*We* aren't. You don't have to say a word if you don't want to. I can do enough talking for both of us."

Jennie chuckled. "I don't doubt that one bit."

She leaned her head against the propped-up pillow, watching Lisa spread a sleeping bag on the floor. "You weren't kidding when you said you stayed here a lot." The sleeping bag had been stored in Jennie's closet along with several pillows. She'd taken a pair of pink jersey pajamas from Jennie's chest of drawers.

"Are you sure you don't live here?" Jennie found it a bit odd that Lisa would know her room better than she did.

"We've grown up together, Jennie." Lisa tossed the pillows on the floor and crawled into the sleeping bag. Fluffing up the pillows, she added, "We're more like sisters than cousins." Her eyes filled with tears.

"What's wrong?"

Lisa used her sleeve to brush them away. "I know this sounds weird, but I miss you. I mean the real you—I mean before you got amnesia."

Jennie didn't know what to say. "Am I that different now?"

"In some ways, no. But before all this happened you were more outspoken. The old you would be trying to figure out what happened. You wouldn't be so afraid." Lisa flashed a teary grin. "You were one of the bravest people I know."

"Were?" Jennie leaned forward. "I lost my memory. I'm not dead."

"There!" Lisa brightened. "Did you hear that?"

"What?"

"That tone. Sounded just like the old you—opinionated and sarcastic."

Jennie screwed up her face. "And you miss that?"

"I suppose it sounds strange, but yeah, I do."

Jennie sighed. "You aren't making much sense. If I'm sarcastic and opinionated why would I have so many friends? You did say I had friends."

"Lots, because you're also very kind. You help people. And if someone is hurting, you're right there for them."

"So I have some good traits."

"Definitely. You're independent. My dad says you're a straight arrow—which means you don't let people talk you into doing things that are wrong or that you don't want to do, like drugs and stuff. You have a mind of your own."

Jennie huffed. "I hope so. If it isn't mine, whose would it be?"

Lisa giggled. "Well, there have been times when your mom's said you weren't in your right mind."

Jennie sobered. "I guess that would be now."

"Oh, I'm sorry. I didn't mean . . ."

"It's okay." Jennie scooted down in bed. Once Lisa had crawled into her sleeping bag, Jennie turned off the light and they said their good-nights.

Jennie stared into the darkness, watching shadowy patterns appear as a soft light crept in through the closed blinds. Though she tried not to think about it, Jennie's thoughts drifted to the isolated cabin in the mountains. She wondered what Lisa would think about her desire to go back. Was it a Jennie thing to do?

After a while Jennie turned onto her side so she was facing her cousin. "Are you still awake?"

"Yeah. I was thinking about ways to help you get your memory back."

"Come up with anything?" Jennie raised herself onto her elbow.

"Swimming."

"Why swimming?"

"Because you love it. Swimming clears your head and helps you figure things out. When you're upset, you swim. It gets you over being mad and upset."

"Hmm. I think I knew that."

"So you want to go swimming tomorrow?"

"Sounds good. Maybe it will help me regain my strength." She hesitated. "This might sound strange, but what I really want to do is go back to the cabin."

"Why?"

"Earlier, Gram told me I should take my intuition seriously, and it's practically screaming at me to go."

"And she's totally right." Lisa's voice rose with excitement. "You've always had a sort of sixth sense. Let's do it. We can go this weekend. I'll bet Scott and Gavin would like to go too."

"Can't. Dad made it very clear that I have to go with an adult. Preferably him or Gram and J.B., or a police officer."

"Rocky. I wonder if he'd be able to take you. Hey, he might let all of us go up with you." Lisa let out a giggle. "Unless of course you'd rather go alone. . . ."

"Very funny." Jennie fluffed her pillow. "But you do have a point. The more of us that go, the safer it will be for me."

"Great. Let's ask Gram about it tomorrow. If she thinks it's a good idea, she'll make it happen."

Jennie inhaled deeply and released her breath slowly. Going to the mountain excited and terrified her. A tight band of apprehension wrapped itself around her chest.

23

At midnight Jennie was still awake. Lisa had been sleeping for at least an hour. While Jennie was bone tired, her mind refused to relax. Over and over she thought about how she would get to the cabin and what might happen there. Threatening, faceless figures haunted her whenever she began to drift off.

The anxiety over what lay ahead had shoved her adrenaline into overdrive. Unable to stand the tormenting half dreams, Jennie sat up and turned on the lamp. She thought about going downstairs to get a snack or glass of milk, but she wasn't sure she could make it. Instead, she lay there letting her gaze drift around the room looking for clues to her past. Lisa shifted and moaned but didn't wake up.

Jennie picked up a book from the lower shelf of the nightstand. If the bookmark was any indication, she'd read almost half of it. Nothing about it looked familiar so Jennie took the bookmark out and started from the beginning. A mystery. She read a page before setting it down, too restless to concentrate.

The doctor said you should write down your feelings.

Not a bad idea. Jennie opened the bedside table drawer and found a stash of pens, some paper, and a journal covered in blue velvet. She leaned back against the pillows and began to examine it, first running her hand over the cloth cover, then opening it.

Jennie's name was written on the first page. According

to the inscription, it had been a gift from Aunt Kate. Jennie opened it and began to read the first entry, which she had made in early November. *"You write in your diary almost every day,"* Mom had told her that first day Jennie had awakened from the coma. That meant there were other journals.

After reading through two entries, she set the journal aside. Even though she had written them Jennie felt as though she were intruding into someone else's deepest thoughts. Her family and friends had convinced her that she was indeed Jennie McGrady, but the thoughts and feelings written in the diary belonged to a stranger.

You are Jennie. They are your thoughts too.

"Are they?" she said quietly. Maybe in time she'd be able to read them and accept them as her own, but not now. She picked up the journal again, and turning to a blank page, she began to write.

> *They tell me my name is Jennie McGrady. They must know. I guess I am her on the outside, but inside I don't know. So much of me is missing. I feel like an actress playing a part. I guess I can learn how to act like her, talk like her, do all the things she used to do, but will I ever really be Jennie? Or will I always feel like an imposter?*
>
> *Coming into the house today I felt like a stranger. I've taken over her room. I'm wearing her clothes, and now I'm even writing in her diary.*
>
> *Everyone tells me to take my time and eventually my memory will come back. But will it? Dad and Rocky think I'm in danger—especially if I'm able to identify the bank robbers. They are out there somewhere. Three of them— maybe more. I'm afraid. I woke up in the woods wounded and terrified. I can't remember how I got there or who . . . Maybe I'd be safer if I didn't remember.*

Panic attacked her again as another image came and went as fast as the flash on a camera. A fist flying toward her face. Once again the picture disappeared before she could grasp it.

She snapped the book shut and set it back in the drawer. It was too soon.

————

"J.B. and I are going home for a few days," Gram announced at breakfast the next morning. Seven of them— Mom, Dad, Gram, J.B., Nick, Scott, and Jennie—had gathered around the large dining room table. Aunt Kate had picked Lisa up at seven since she had to get ready for school. "We're wondering what you would think about sending Jennie with us. We can bring her back in about a week."

"It'd do her a world of good," J.B. added in his smooth Irish brogue. "Give her a chance to rest and recuperate."

"I don't think so." Mom picked up half of a toasted muffin and reached for the butter. "The doctor wants her to come in at least every other day for a week or so. And she'll need to get back to school soon." She glanced at Jennie. "Besides, I'm not ready for her to leave yet."

Gram looked disappointed. "I understand. I just wish we didn't have to go home, but J.B. and I both have urgent business we need to take care of."

"I'd like to go," Jennie said. Her bravado about going back up the mountain had waned after having another flashback. If the flashbacks were this terrible, what would it be like to remember everything? She didn't want to know any more. *You really don't have to remember,* she told herself. *You can pick up from here and just go on. Maybe if the bank robbers know you can't remember, they'll leave you alone.*

"We'll all go down soon, princess." Dad passed on the plate of bacon and helped himself to the French toast. "But your mom's right. You need to be here."

Since both parents seemed adamant, Jennie didn't argue. Instead, she fixed her eyes on her still-empty plate. When the bacon came around she took two pieces and passed the platter to Scott.

"I have to head home today too," Scott told them. "Either that or I lose my job."

Jennie glanced up at him. He didn't seem too disappointed. But then, she hadn't been very good company. "When did you talk to them?"

"My boss called last night after you went to bed." He shrugged. "I'd like to stay, but . . ."

"We appreciate your staying as long as you have, Scott," Mom said. "You've been a big help."

He shrugged and gave Nick a wink. "Nick's a great kid. You can call on me to baby-sit anytime."

"I don't want Scott to go." Nick reached for his milk. "Him and me is buddies."

"*He* and *I are* buddies," Mom interjected.

"That's what I said."

Jennie felt a stab of jealousy at the camaraderie between the two of them. She still felt as bereft and disconnected as she had during the night. Like she didn't quite belong.

"Can he take me for a ride on his motorcycle?" Nick asked. "He promised."

"Whoa! Not so fast." Scott paused his fork in midair. "You trying to get me in trouble or something? I just said you could sit on it while I walk it around the driveway."

Dad laughed. "I think we can handle that."

"Yay!" Nick cheered. "Let's go right after breakfast."

"You got it." Scott held up his hand, and Nick slapped it in an exuberant high-five.

"You don't mind, do you, Jennie?" Scott turned to her.

"Mind?" Jennie left her musings and focused on his eyes a moment before looking away. "Um . . . no. I guess not."

"Good. I'd like to talk to you later—before I head out. Maybe we could take a walk in the park or something." He drained his glass of milk.

"Sure." Jennie flashed him a smile. "I mean, if it's okay with my parents."

"If Jennie can handle it I see no reason why she shouldn't." Looking at Dad, Mom added, "Do you think it will be safe?"

"I'll call Rocky or one of the other guys before I go in

to work. I don't mind her going out, but I want someone with her." He gave Gram a knowing look. "We checked around the neighborhood last night. No one knew anything about the car Jennie saw. It could have just been someone driving by, but we aren't taking any chances."

Jennie's heart jumped to her throat. "M-maybe a walk isn't such a good idea."

Her parents looked at each other as if to say, "This isn't the Jennie we know."

From what she'd heard about herself, she'd had a lot more courage.

"Sweetheart . . ." Gram hesitated. "It's understandable that you'd be afraid, but you can't hide in the house forever."

Mom sighed and closed her eyes. "As much as I'd like to protect you and keep you safe, your grandmother is right. You can't put your life on hold. We don't know that they're anywhere around. Those bank robbers could be out of the country by now, and here we are, practically quivering in our shoes." The whole idea seemed to energize her. "We don't know what will happen from one moment to the next, and I won't have us all afraid to walk out the door for fear someone will gun us down—or something equally horrid."

"Well said, Susan." J.B. lifted his orange juice glass in a salute.

Dad looked like he wanted to applaud her. "The chances of that happening are slim. Still, it pays to be cautious."

Gram nodded. "God is not the author of fear, and Susan is right. We can't let it control our lives. On the other hand we need to use common sense." Turning to Jennie, she said, "What do you think of all this, darling?"

"I . . . I'm not sure. Part of me wants to just crawl under the covers and stay there. But I don't think I could do that." She told them about the terrible night she'd had. "I want it to be over with. I want the bank robbers caught and . . ."

"They will be eventually," Dad assured her.

"Yes, but if I could remember, it might happen sooner."

"You can't rush the healing, Jennie," Gram reminded her. "Be patient. Trust the Lord to bring out what you need when you need it."

"That's excellent advice, princess." Dad backed his chair up and placed his napkin on the table. "We all need to trust that God will work this out in the end. We need more prayer and less worry."

When they'd finished breakfast Dad left for work. Scott and Nick went outside for Nick's bike ride.

"We'll take care of those," Gram offered when Mom started clearing the dishes. "You just sit down and give orders."

"Thanks." Mom set down the dishes she was holding, then turned around and gave Gram and J.B. hugs. "I honestly don't know what I would have done without you two. These last few days . . ."

"I'm just sorry we can't stay. I've talked to Kate, and she'll come over later to clean. Jennie will be able to help before you know it."

"I could now." Jennie began rinsing and placing dishes in the dishwasher while Gram and J.B. cleared the table. Mom settled on the couch with her feet up.

"Gram?" Jennie dried her hands.

"Yes?"

"I wish I could go with you."

Gram wrapped an arm around Jennie's shoulders. "I wish you could too. But it's better that you stay. Like your mother said . . ."

"I know. I have to see the doctor."

"Ye'll be coming to the coast before you know it." J.B. cupped her chin and turned her face up to look into his sky-blue eyes. "And don't you be worrying about your memory, lass. It'll come around in time."

"I hope so."

Scott came in with Nick following close behind. "Ride's over. Are you ready for that walk?"

"Can I go too?" Nick grabbed Scott around the leg.

"Nick, old chap." J.B. sat on the chair and patted his leg, and Nick climbed into his lap. "How about staying here with your papa and Gram for a while. You promised you'd read to us. Or have you forgotten how already?"

"I haven't forgotten."

"Well, then. Why don't you get your book and show us?"

"Okay." Nick scrambled down and scampered off to his room.

Scott tossed him a grateful look and grabbed Jennie's hand. "Come on. Let's go."

They were just heading out the door when a van pulled up in front. A thin, wiry woman with curly blond hair got out, then opened the rear door. Pulling out a bouquet of flowers, she started up the walk.

"Can we help you?" Scott asked.

The woman smiled. "I've got some flowers for Jennie McGrady. Is she home?"

"I'm Jennie."

"Well, then, here you go." As she handed the bouquet over, Jennie caught a whiff of stale cigarettes. Her heart raced as it always seemed to when she picked up on that scent. Startled, Jennie staggered back, clutching at Scott's shirt sleeve.

"Jennie? What's wrong?"

Her mind flashed back to an image of her raising her arms to ward off a blow.

"Is she all right?" the delivery person asked. "Maybe you'd better sit down."

"No, I'll be okay. Just . . . nothing." The image was gone again. Like the others, it had come and gone too quickly to grasp details. Jennie held her hand against her forehead and took several deep breaths.

"She gets these flashbacks," Scott explained.

"Is there anything I can do to help?"

"I don't think so. Um . . . are you a friend or something?"

"Oh no. Just delivering these. There's a card."

"Thanks. I'd better take her back inside."

"Good idea. You take care of yourself." The woman got back into the van and drove off.

Scott took the flowers out of Jennie's hand. She leaned against him as he brought her to the stairs. Collapsing on them, she hugged the railing. "Maybe a walk isn't such a good idea. I never know when it's going to happen. It's embarrassing."

"You don't have to be embarrassed, Jen. Try to relax."

"I am." After a few moments her pulse rate settled into its normal rhythm. "I never know when it's going to hit me. This one was awful."

"What triggered it?"

Jennie frowned, trying to remember. "Every time I smell cigarettes on someone, I start feeling panicky." She brightened. "That's something, isn't it? I'll bet the bank robbers smoke."

"Well . . ." Scott grinned. "That narrows the odds by about sixty percent."

"Cute."

He winked. "I like to think so."

Jennie got to her feet and dusted off her pants. "We'd better take these inside."

Jennie set the arrangement on the dining room table and looked for a card. There wasn't one. "That's funny. The lady said it was here."

"Maybe it fell off."

"Must have."

Gram came into the dining room. "Hi. I thought you two had gone for a walk."

"We got as far as the sidewalk," Scott said. "Jennie got some flowers."

"How nice. Who are they from?"

"Don't know. The card's missing."

"We should be able to find out easily enough. Did you notice which florist delivered them?"

"No." Jennie tried to picture the van and driver. "There wasn't a logo on it."

"What did the courier say?"

"Just that she had a delivery for me and that the card was attached."

Scott told Gram about the flashback and what had triggered it.

"I see." She eyed the floral arrangement with suspicion.

"What's wrong?" Scott asked. "You think there might be a bomb in it or something?"

"What's this about a bomb?" J.B. came in from the kitchen, adjusting the cuffs on his shirt.

Gram told him about the flowers. "Let's have a look."

Five minutes later J.B. came back inside. He'd taken the flower arrangement outdoors to dismantle it. "All clear. Nothing to worry about."

"I don't like it," Gram said. "A delivery van without a logo. Jennie's reaction to her. If you see the woman or her van again, Jennie, report it immediately."

Jennie promised she would. Another huge lump formed in the pit of her stomach. Could the woman have been more than she seemed?

Not wanting to think about the possibilities, Jennie grabbed Scott's hand and pulled him toward the door.

"I think I'm ready for that walk now."

Rocky was parked at the curb and seemed annoyed when they told him where they were going. He walked beside them the several blocks to the park, then stayed a short distance away to give them the privacy Scott asked for. They wandered along the paths inside the Crystal Springs Rhododendron Garden. The air held a promise of the coming winter. Jennie was glad she'd chosen to wear a warm sweater and turtleneck. Come spring the garden would be full of blooms. Now it was littered with brown soggy leaves from an overnight rain.

Jennie remembered the leaves in the woods and how Lucy had stirred them up as she paced back and forth. Another memory slipped in. She was lying on the ground again.

Crunching leaves. Birds chattering.

"Stupid girl," a man said. *"I was going to let you live. Then you had to go and kill yourself."*

Jennie stopped. The memory, if that's what it was, had a different feel to it than the others. There was no overwhelming sense of panic.

"You okay? Maybe we shouldn't have come this far."

"No, it's okay. Let's sit here for a minute." Jennie lowered herself onto one of the benches that looked out over the small lake. Ducks and geese hurriedly swam away, then edged their way back, apparently looking for handouts.

"Are you sure you're doing okay?"

Jennie told him about the scene and the man's voice. "He said he wasn't going to kill me. He must have thought I was dead."

"Who?"

"The man in the woods."

"Can you describe him?"

"No. I was . . ." Jennie almost said "dead." She shuddered thinking how close she must have come.

Brakes whined as a bus driver pulled into the parking lot. Moments later at least a dozen senior citizens filed into the park. Some had cameras, some walkers, others had canes.

"Looks like we have company."

"It's a popular place."

Scott leaned forward. "Want to walk some more?"

"No. I should get back."

"What was that?" Scott pointed to a spot across the water.

"I don't see anything."

"I could have sworn I saw someone in the bushes over there."

The leaves on a large rhododendron were still swaying. The hairs on the back of Jennie's neck stood on end.

"I'd blame it on the wind, but there is none."

"I think we'd better go." Jennie turned to tell Rocky, but he was gone.

24

"I know the flashbacks are upsetting to you, Jennie, but they can be helpful." Dr. Mason shined the light in Jennie's eyes, examining one, then the other. "It might help to think of them as puzzle pieces. Each time it happens you get a little more insight into your past. Have you been writing them down?"

"Yes, but they come and go so fast."

"What about the triggers?"

"That's harder. Sometimes it's a smell—like cigarette smoke—or a word or a place. Sometimes it just happens and it doesn't feel like there's a connection."

"How often are you having them?"

Jennie closed her eyes. "About the same—two or three times a day."

"Well, Jennie"—he picked up her chart—"physically you're doing very well. How would you feel about going back to school Monday?"

"I'm not sure." Jennie told him about the flower-delivery incident and the outing to the park with Scott on Friday and about how paranoid she'd become. Rocky had seen the movement in the rhododendron, as well, and had gone to investigate. A false alarm, he'd said. The only person close to the plant in question had been an elderly woman with a walker. "I'm afraid whoever hurt me is still out there somewhere." Despite her efforts to be brave, Jennie still felt vulnerable and threatened.

"You have good reason to be concerned. Your father mentioned that he'd been keeping an especially close watch on you. Why don't you talk with your parents about it? I think being in school and into your old routine will help in your adjustment."

Jennie agreed. As her mother had said, she couldn't go on worrying forever about the possibility that her enemy would strike again.

That afternoon the sheriff came by to let Jennie know she could have her car back. Dad took her to pick it up at the impound lot and followed her home. During the entire trip Jennie felt as though a huge rubber band had been wrapped around her chest. Twice she had a flashback of a man with balding hair firing his gun at her. When another flashback started Jennie gripped the steering wheel and pulled over to the side of the road. Dad pulled in right behind her.

"What's wrong, princess?"

She told him about the flashbacks. "They're really scary, Dad, but I think I'd recognize the man who tried to kill me."

"That's great, Jennie." He grinned. "What do you say we get your car home, and I'll take you downtown to give our artist a description. The sooner we get the guy's picture out to the public, the better."

Dad squeezed her shoulder. "You doing okay driving?"

Jennie nodded and before long was back in the traffic.

The six-o'clock news team talked about Jennie, went over the case, and showed the face of the man she'd seen in the flashbacks. Jennie had no idea whether the face she'd seen was real or one she'd dreamed up.

On Monday morning Jennie drove to school. It was the first time she'd been alone since the accident. She'd visited the school over the weekend and joined the swim team in practice on Saturday. Her father had taken her both ways. The danger of Jennie being attacked at this point seemed nil, since there had been no real threats or attacks on her life. The bank robbers had made no further hits in the area, and police suspected they'd headed south. There had been two robberies in the Bend and Redmond area and another in Eureka, California. Still, Dad reminded her that it was too soon to let down her guard. "You can go, princess, but watch your back."

"Don't worry." She kissed her parents good-bye and headed out, scared but determined not to let her fears take over. *"Trust God,"* Gram had said. And Jennie planned to do just that. Since she'd missed so much school, Mom suggested she stay for all the classes for a few days to get caught up before going back to her homeschool status.

School proved beneficial in a number of ways. The teachers and students treated her as one of them. Jennie enjoyed every class and found her spirits rising as the day progressed. By the afternoon, she was almost feeling normal.

When school got out she was exhausted but decided to go to swim practice anyway. She had the feeling that swimming would relax her and allow her to remember. Jennie saw herself swimming with the dolphins again.

The doctor had been right; going to school and swimming was beginning to pay off. She began to recall her family and friends. Lisa had come to swim practice, and Jennie could hardly wait to tell her. She'd be dropping Lisa off at her house, and though it seemed a small thing, Jennie knew exactly where Lisa lived.

She celebrated her good news with Aunt Kate and called her mother. Mom promised to call Dr. Mason.

On the way home Jennie couldn't stop smiling. Though there were lapses in her memory, things were coming together.

But not everything, Jennie reminded herself. *You still don't remember what happened out in those woods. You don't know how you got all those bruises or the bullet in your leg.*

Fear pushed away her sense of achievement and joy. They were out there somewhere. Maybe they'd moved on and forgotten all about her. Maybe they didn't know they hadn't killed her. Of course, with all the publicity . . . She wished she could be sure.

Feeling apprehensive again, Jennie glanced in the rearview mirror to reassure herself that Rocky was still behind her. He wasn't. Then she remembered. Once she'd gotten to Lisa's house, she'd told him he didn't have to hang around. She could see that he was exhausted from the long day. She promised to call him when she got home. He'd put up an argument at first, but after talking to Jennie's dad, Rocky agreed to call it a day.

The traffic was heavy as usual, but she saw nothing out of the ordinary. "You're being paranoid again," she told herself. "You're almost home. Nothing to worry about."

Jennie put on her turn signal to exit the freeway on the ramp near her home. Glancing into her rearview mirror, she saw a white newer-model car tailgating her. She grumbled, then started to move into the right lane to take the exit. The white car whipped into the right lane and pulled right beside her, cutting her off.

Everything happened at once. Jennie spotted a gun. She slammed on her brakes. Tires screeched. The passenger-side window shattered. Jennie cranked the steering wheel left. Screeching wheels ended in a crunch as her Mustang collided with the vehicle in the middle lane.

25

The air bag popped out, slamming Jennie against the seat. For a moment she thought she would suffocate. But just as quickly the air bag released, leaving Jennie covered with a fine powder and making it nearly impossible to breathe. She coughed and gasped for breath until the powder settled.

Once the coughing stopped, reality set in. She hadn't been injured—at least not that she could tell. The driver's-side window had imploded. Glass shards lay across her lap.

Peering through the sharp, jagged glass still adhered to the window frame, she could see the damage. The front passenger side of the expensive-looking car she'd hit had imbedded itself into the front driver's side of her Mustang. The driver, a man in a business suit, still had a cell phone in his hand. Chalky gray powder covered his dark hair, face, and clothing. He stared straight ahead as if he couldn't quite believe what had happened. Then he crumpled, his head lolling forward and hitting the deflated air bag.

He's hurt. Jennie reached for the door handle. She had to get to him. Wedged against the other car, her door wouldn't budge. Her hand shook as she brought it back to the bent steering wheel. Even if she had been able to open the door, it would have done her no good. Her left leg was wedged in the twisted wreckage.

Feeling nauseated, Jennie leaned back against the seat.

"Hey!" A man with a scruffy gray beard pounded at the passenger side. The already shattered glass caved in, tinkling like wind chimes as the shards bounced against one another. "You okay in there?"

"I . . . I think so." Fresh air wafted in, stirring up the dust.

"Stay put!" the man ordered. "I've called 9-1-1. They should be here soon."

"The man in the other car . . ." She coughed again, batting her hand against the annoying powder. "He's hurt."

"There's another guy checking on him. You just take it easy. You'll be out of there in no time."

Take it easy? As if she'd ever be able to do that again. The crazy woman driver had tried to kill her. A number of people had stopped to help. Everyone seemed to be talking at once.

"Anybody hurt?"

"What happened?"

"Kid crossed the lane."

"I thought I heard a gunshot."

"Anybody hit?"

"Anybody else hear a shot?"

"I did. Did you see who did it?"

That's what Jennie wanted to know. The woman had been wearing sunglasses. It had happened so fast. Had it been a random shooting? A case of road rage? Or had the woman deliberately singled her out? Was this somehow connected with the bank robbers?

Sirens interrupted her thoughts, and before long Jennie was in an ambulance on her way to the hospital—again.

Two hours later Jennie still lay in the ER on a stretcher, watching the hospital staff scurrying back and forth between patients. Most of her injuries were minor. Though the bullet had missed her, the accident itself had resulted in a number of cuts. Her left leg was bruised but not broken. If it hadn't been for her recent head injury, the doctor might have let her go home. But the impact of the crash had thrown her against the headrest and caused a nasty headache and more swelling. Dr. Mason insisted she stay for a couple of days so he could run some tests and observe her.

A state patrol officer had come in to question her shortly after her arrival at the hospital. "Sounds like another case of road rage," he said after hearing her take on the accident.

"It definitely wasn't road rage." Jennie then told him about her encounter with the bank robbers.

"And you think there's a connection?"

"The woman set me up. When she saw I was turning off she zipped around on my right and blocked my exit. Next thing I knew she pulled out a gun and fired."

"People do all kinds of crazy things on the road."

"Yes, but I think she was just after me."

The officer asked a few more questions, then said, "We've got a number of witnesses. Hopefully we'll be able to piece together what happened out there. And track down the woman responsible."

"Is the man I hit okay?"

"Shaken up. You were both very lucky."

Jennie didn't feel lucky. She felt plagued and very afraid. Her parents' arrival did nothing to ease her fears. After their initial hugs and kisses and reassurances, Dad had gone to make some phone calls. Mom sat down next to her, furiously knitting a baby afghan. Worry etched her face. Every once in a while she'd wince as if in pain.

Jennie felt guilty over being so much trouble. Mom needed rest and wasn't getting it. "Mom, why don't you have Dad take you home? You shouldn't be here."

Mom looked up, a puzzled, blank look in her eyes. Her face had gone a pasty white. Jennie's heart plunged.

Mom clutched at her stomach. A knitting needle clattered to the floor.

"Mom!"

26

"Is she going to be okay?" Jennie asked for the ump-teenth time. Within a few minutes after the nurses had picked her mother off the floor, Jennie had been transferred to a hospital room. That had been two hours ago, and this was the first she'd seen of her father since her mother's collapse. The nurses had no answers. All they could tell her was that the doctors were doing all they could and that she would just have to be patient. Jennie was tired of having people tell her to relax or be patient. She had very little patience and a lot of frustration.

"We don't know yet, Jennie." Dad dragged a hand through his hair. He looked worn-out and badly in need of a shave. "They've admitted her and are running more tests now."

"I wish I could go see her."

"You will. Soon. When the doctor says it's okay, I'll come get you."

"They should have put her in here with me."

Dad didn't comment. They both knew she needed to be in the obstetrics and gynecology ward, which, unfortunately, was in another wing.

"You should be with her," Jennie said. "She needs you more than I do."

"I know." He sighed heavily. "Jennie, there's something . . ."

Jennie didn't need the words. She knew in her heart

why he'd come in to see her. She had seen it in his expression from the moment he walked into the room. "It's the baby, isn't it?"

He nodded, tears pooling in his deep blue eyes. "We lost her."

"It was a girl?" Jennie waited for her own tears, but they didn't come. Instead, a strange numbness engulfed her. The grief she wanted to feel for the loss of her baby sister simply wasn't there. And Jennie knew why. Though she'd come to accept these people as her family, she didn't really know them. She had no real attachment to any of them. More than ever Jennie felt like an outsider. As much as she wanted to share her father's grief, she couldn't. At least not in her heart, where it counted.

He wiped his eyes with the heels of his hands. "She didn't have Down's syndrome like the doctor's thought she might. She was perfectly normal."

"Then, why?"

"We don't know." He wrapped his arms around Jennie. "I need to get back. Right now I wish there were two of me."

"It's okay. I'll be fine."

"That's what you said before the accident. Rocky should be here any minute."

"Rocky? Why?"

"I don't want you left alone. We're not making the same mistake again."

"Oh, right." Concern for her mother had overridden her awareness of her own precarious situation.

"He offered to look after you until your grandmother gets here."

"Gram's coming back?" Relief flooded her. Somehow she felt Gram would be able to make everything okay.

"She's on her way." Dad seemed to regain his composure. "Should be here within a couple hours."

"Good."

Dad hesitated. "I should stay. . . ."

"No, you shouldn't. You should be with Mom. I'll be okay."

"I'll tell the nurses to be especially watchful."

When he was gone she lay there, still numb, allowing the events of the past few days to play through her mind. It had grown dark outside, but Jennie didn't bother turning on the light. With every footstep she heard, with every voice, her fears grew. She was alone. Why hadn't Rocky come? A noise in the hallway chased the thoughts away and set her heart to hammering even more.

"Rocky, where are you?" She clasped her hands and offered up a prayer.

Margaret, the same nurse who'd admitted her, came around the curtain. Jennie practically jumped out of the bed.

"How's it going?"

"Okay." Jennie's relief came out in a heavy sigh.

Margaret turned on the light over the bed and stuck a thermometer in Jennie's mouth. "I hate these short days, don't you?"

"Hmm." Jennie nodded in agreement.

For the next few minutes the nurse concentrated on taking Jennie's vital signs and making notes on the chart. After checking her pupils she gave Jennie a sympathetic smile. "Everything looks good."

"Does that mean I can go see my mother?"

She gave Jennie a stern look. "You don't quit, do you?"

"I . . . she lost her baby. I'd like to see her."

"Oh no. I'm so sorry. Of course you can go. Dr. Mason said you could be up and around as long as you don't put any weight on that leg. In fact, I have some crutches for you to use."

"Great. Bring me the crutches and point me in the right direction."

"Whoa." She chuckled. "Not so fast. I'll call the ob-gyn floor and ask if it's okay. If so, we'll have an orderly take you over in a wheelchair."

"But I thought you said I could use crutches."

"Yes, to walk to the bathroom and back and up and down the hall. Not to go all over the hospital."

While Jennie waited she leaned back again and closed her eyes. She was tired. *When is it going to end?* Her mother had blamed herself for Jennie's abduction. Now Jennie blamed herself. Why had she gone on that hike? From what Lisa and her parents had told her, she'd insisted on going even though she'd had to drive up the mountain alone to wait for them. If she hadn't gone, she'd never have been abducted. She wouldn't have lost her memory. Mom wouldn't have been so worried, and she and the baby would both be okay.

You don't know that, an inner voice seemed to say. Not wanting to think about her assumed guilt, Jennie opened her eyes and turned on the television set suspended from the ceiling. The evening news was just coming on. Jennie's picture filled the screen as the reporter talked about the accident.

"A case of road rage, or an attack by her abductors?" The news anchor went on to give details of the accident and reviewed the history of Jennie's abduction. "Sources close to the family have told us that Jennie is back in school and feels it's only a matter of time before she regains her memory. We certainly hope she does."

"As do the police," the other anchor added. "They believe Ms. McGrady holds key evidence that could break this case wide open."

"Don't remind me." Jennie pressed the Power button on the remote. "I wonder who those 'sources' are." A strong and compelling sense of urgency settled over her. Had the people who'd wanted her dead heard the news story? Had the woman in the car meant to kill her? Now they would know they had failed. Would they try again?

"Where is that orderly?" She pressed the call button. "And why isn't Rocky here yet?" He should have been there by now. Dad didn't want her left alone.

Fear crept in again. Had something happened to him? She ran her fingers through her hair as she heard footsteps in the hall. It sounded like they stopped at the door to her room. A curtain hid her view.

"Is someone there?"

"Just me." Margaret came in with a pair of crutches.

"I thought you were getting someone to take me over to see my mother."

"I'm sorry. I called. Sometimes it takes a while. We're short staffed—as usual. I'll call again."

Margaret got Jennie out of bed, adjusted the crutches, and showed her how to use them properly. After promising to call for a volunteer or an orderly to bring a wheelchair, she left.

Minutes later Jennie heard footsteps again. They seemed to stop at her door.

"Hello? Anyone there?"

No one answered. Jennie eased out of bed, got her crutches, and pushed the curtain aside. Her heart raced with expectation. She wouldn't have been at all surprised to find the woman who'd shot at her on the freeway, but there was no one. She crept to the door and looked out into the hall.

"Can I help you?" One of the nurses was coming out of another room and saw her.

"No," Jennie answered. "I was just going to the bathroom." Feeling foolish, she used the small bathroom and went back to bed. She had to stop being such a pathetic wimp.

Unfortunately, the only cure she could see for the paranoia she felt was getting her memory back. All she had were the flashbacks and what she'd read or been told about the robberies and her abduction. Maybe if she wrote everything down again . . .

Dr. Mason had been right. The more often the flashbacks came, the more details she was able to pick up. Jennie called the nurse and asked for some paper and a pen. Margaret responded quickly and Jennie began making notes, listing as many details as she could remember about the woman who'd delivered flowers and the one who'd shot at her. She then wrote down each incident where she'd experienced the flashbacks. Gram had told her to trust her intuition, so Jennie also scribbled down each person she'd felt uncomfortable with, including those she'd seen in the hospital.

Writing things down helped to give her perspective. Instead of letting the events frighten her, she was determined to use logic and fact. She realized that she'd learned a great deal over the past few days. She'd witnessed a bank robbery and given descriptions to the police. Though she didn't remember the event, the papers had been full of information. There had been three bank robbers. There had also been three people besides herself in the cabin. In her flashbacks, the man was always holding a gun. She felt certain she'd know him if she saw him.

Unfortunately, none of the people who'd set off her inner warnings fit the thin, balding man she pictured. The male housekeeper she'd been uncomfortable with had been young. Any one of the three bank robbers—or all of them—might be after her, and with their disguises, how could she know? Even if her memory came back, one of them could walk into her room and she wouldn't have a clue.

Fifteen minutes had passed and still no wheelchair. And no Rocky. There would be no point in calling the nurse again. They'd just tell her to be patient. *Grrr.* She was so tired of hearing that. Tired of waiting. Tired of not being able to remember. Tired of living in fear.

Heaving a sigh, Jennie set the pad aside, settled back against the pillows, and closed her eyes. It all seemed pointless. What good would it do to remember if she couldn't recognize them anyway? At the moment she didn't feel like remembering. Nor did she feel like seeing her mother. What would she say? How do you console someone who's just lost her baby? So what if her attempted killers came back to finish the job? Let them. Right now she didn't care. And there wasn't much she could do anyway. All she wanted to do was sleep. With any luck at all, everything she'd experienced these past few days would be a bad dream. She'd wake up and everything would be okay.

Her grandmother had told her to trust God. Maybe that's what she needed to do. *"Come unto me . . . and I will give you rest. . . . Don't be afraid."* The familiar Bible verses came to mind, and Jennie clung to them. She captured a picture she'd seen of Jesus sitting with children and imagined herself as a small child climbing onto His lap. Warmth and light seemed to fill her being as she felt herself drifting off.

Though she hadn't been able to see the woman in the car all that clearly, Jennie suspected the flower lady may have changed cars and put on a different disguise. That fit with what she'd learned about the robbers changing cars, and she figured that was why she'd been abducted in the first place—the man needed her car.

With her eyes still closed she tried to picture the hands of the housekeepers and other staff members who'd come in. Jennie couldn't remember seeing rings, but she hadn't really paid that much attention to their hands. She'd been too busy studying their faces. Julie, the nurse who'd said she worked in the emergency room, came to mind. She was a smoker, and the scent had triggered several flashbacks. Was she for real? Maybe it was time to check her out.

Simple enough. She'd just go down to the ER and ask. Jennie got out of bed, slipped into the striped cotton hospital robe and hospital-issue nonskid socks, grabbed her crutches, and headed out the door.

Margaret smiled as she came down the hall toward her. "I called again for someone, Jennie, but the orderlies are all tied up and we don't have anyone on volunteer duty. I'd take you myself, but . . . ." She shrugged. "I just don't have time."

"Um . . . that's okay."

"You seem to be doing well with those crutches."

"Yeah."

"Well, don't overdo it." She tossed her hair back over her shoulder as she hurried into one of the rooms.

A ward secretary gave Jennie a cursory glance as she

made her way past the nurses' station. Moments later she was standing in front of the elevator, feeling guilty about sneaking away.

The elevator doors swished open. Jennie hesitated, then turned around and headed back to her room. She'd no sooner gotten settled back in her bed when the wheelchair person showed up. "You Jennie McGrady?"

"Yes."

"Sorry to take so long. Busy night. Got orders to take you to the ob-gyn floor." The man was tall and muscular and smelled as though he'd just smoked a cigarette.

The alarms went off in Jennie's head. "I changed my mind. I don't need the wheelchair after all."

27

Margaret came into the room, looking worried. "What's wrong, Jennie? Steve says you changed your mind."

Jennie wished she could disappear into the mattress. *"Trust your instincts,"* Gram had said. Well, she had and they were wrong. Steve was obviously a legitimate hospital employee. She deliberated over whether or not to come clean. She could just say she wasn't feeling well but then decided she may as well be honest about it. "Um . . . I was afraid to go with him. I had this feeling—like a voice telling me not to go."

"Ah." The nurse gave her an understanding nod. "Well, you don't have to go, but Steve has worked here for ten years. He may have the shape of a linebacker, but he's gentle as a puppy. I asked him to wait. What would you like to do?"

"He probably thinks I'm a nut case."

"I doubt that. Why don't you go? I have a feeling your mother would welcome a visit."

"So it's okay with her doctor?"

"More than okay. He thinks it's a great idea."

"All right." Jennie still discerned that sense of foreboding but pushed it aside. Steve could be trusted, and she doubted he'd let anything happen to her. And since Rocky hadn't shown up . . . Jennie wondered again what could have happened to him.

Before she could think on it any further, Steve came back into the room. "Hey, Jennie, you ready to go?" He was smiling.

"I'm sorry about . . ."

"Hey, no problem. With all that's happened to you, I don't blame you for being cautious." He efficiently helped her into the wheelchair and tucked the crutches along beside her in case she wanted to walk around in her mother's room.

Knowing Steve was legitimate did nothing to ease Jennie's apprehensions over going off the floor with him. The alarm bells continued going off as he pressed the button for the elevator. *Trust your instincts.* As much as Jennie wanted to tell him she'd changed her mind again, she didn't. Instead, she kept telling herself to quit acting like a baby. In no time at all, she'd be in her mother's room and safely seated near her father. Nothing was going to happen. Besides, no one in their right mind would try to hurt her while she was in the hospital corridors. Especially with a big guy like Steve.

The elevator doors opened.

Don't get on the elevator. Jennie's heart tripped as panic drained the color from her face. A woman in green scrubs wielding a stretcher started to get off. "Whoops, wrong floor." She gave Steve a smile and glanced at a bespectacled man with a clerical collar. The priest stood near the panel opposite the stretcher.

Before Jennie could get a good look at them, Steve spun her around and backed her in, then reached around and pressed the button for the second floor. "What floor did you want?" he asked the woman with the stretcher.

"Second." She gave a raspy laugh. "Must have pushed the wrong button. Daydreaming, I guess."

"I know how that goes."

Jennie recognized the woman's voice immediately. No wonder the alarms had gone off in her head. It was the woman who'd delivered the flowers.

The elevator doors closed, trapping them inside. Jennie

swallowed back a cry of alarm. The woman hadn't pushed the wrong button. She'd been planning to get off on the sixth floor. The empty stretcher had probably been meant for her. Then seeing Jennie, she'd had to backtrack. *Gram was right. You should have listened to your intuition.*

Too late now. Jennie swallowed back the overwhelming sense of panic. She needed to think. To find some way to let Steve know this woman was dangerous. But how?

"Hey!" Steve exclaimed. "What's going on? What are you doing with that gun?"

"That should be obvious. This elevator has just been hijacked. Jon, hit the button for the ground floor," she ordered.

"But it'll open on the second. What do we do then?" The man Jennie had thought was a priest leaned forward to do as she'd said. Jennie caught sight of the gun gripped firmly in his right hand. Her gaze shot up to his face, certain he'd be the man she'd envisioned in her flashbacks. He wasn't. This guy was wearing glasses and had brown wavy hair.

Disguises.

"Well, that's up to our passengers," said the woman. Jennie turned toward her. She'd moved out from behind the stretcher and stood next to Steve. Giving Jennie a dark, menacing look, she jabbed her gun into Steve's ribs. "Either of you makes a sound and you'll both be dead."

"What's going on?" Steve glanced back at the woman.

"Just shut your mouth. Do as you're told and no one gets hurt."

Jennie wouldn't have needed her memory to know these were the people who'd abducted her and held her captive in that mountain cabin. She should have recognized Maude the moment the elevator doors opened. Perhaps on one level she had. Jennie wasn't certain when it had happened, but her memory had returned.

"You'd better do as she says," Jennie heard herself say. "They're ruthless."

"Good advice." This came from Jon.

"You know these people?" Steve still sounded shocked and unsure.

"Yeah." Jennie found her voice was surprisingly strong. "You might say that."

The elevator had stopped at the fourth floor. A woman holding a toddler started to get on. From her vantage point, Jennie doubted she could see the guns or know anything was wrong. She held her breath, praying the woman wouldn't try to squeeze in.

The young woman smiled at Jennie, then her baby. "Looks like they're full, sweetie. We'll have to wait for the next one."

The doors closed, and Jennie released the breath she'd been holding. In a couple seconds they'd be on the second floor, then the ground. Then who knew where? Not that it really mattered. Jennie had no doubt she and Steve would both end up dead.

She had to do something—and fast. Jennie glanced down at the crutches tucked beside her. If she could create a diversion . . . Maybe she'd be able to hit the emergency button on the elevator panel. But would that be enough? She and Steve might not make it out alive, but maybe . . .

The elevator dinged its arrival at the second floor. Jennie carefully dislodged one of the crutches with her foot and let it slide. The doors opened. Jennie kicked the crutch forward, and it clattered to the floor. At the same time, she grabbed the wheels of her chair and with as much strength as she could muster backed it into Steve, forcing him into Maude.

Maude's gun went off.

28

The shot sounded like a huge explosion. Jon ducked. The elevator doors closed, hit Jennie's crutch, then snapped open again. As they did, Jennie pressed the emergency button, then dove out. She hit the floor and rolled to the side, landing on a man's shiny black shoes. "Get the police," she shouted above the noisy alarm. Rolling onto her back, she realized that the shoes belonged to her father. "Dad, am I glad to see you."

"Are you okay?" He knelt down beside her.

"Yes. But they'll get away. They've got guns."

"So I heard." He straightened and simultaneously grabbed his cell phone in his left hand, his gun in his right. "Stay down!" Dad yelled to her as well as to the two staff members heading toward them. "Call security. You"—he directed the order to Jennie—"stay put." Then stepping over her, he called for backup.

The door opened and closed on Jennie's crutch again and again. With his back to the wall near the elevator, Dad yelled, "Police! Put your guns on the floor and come out with your hands up."

"It's okay," Steve yelled back. "Don't shoot. I've got them."

Jennie scrambled to her feet, smiling. "It's Steve." She came up behind her father. "He's the orderly."

"Out you go," Steve said. "Now move before I have to use this thing on you."

Jon stepped out of the elevator first, his hands held high. "I didn't do nothing. It was all her idea. I never wanted to kill anybody."

"You stupid fool!" Maude had her arms folded. "You were supposed to be watching her."

"How was I to know she'd throw her crutch out?"

"She's smart. You should never have taken her to the cabin. You should have killed her when you took her car."

"You're both under arrest." Dad informed them of their legal rights as he cuffed them.

Jennie leaned against the wall feeling as if she'd run a marathon.

"Better get you back in the wheelchair." Steve rescued the chair and the crutch from the still-clanging elevator and settled her into it.

"I hope I didn't hurt you, slamming into you like that, but . . ."

"You surprised me for sure. Spurred me into action, really. I was about to do something like that myself when I saw what you were doing with that crutch."

"What happened?"

Steve's chest seemed to broaden as he spoke. "I jabbed her in the gut with my elbow and pushed her gun arm up. It discharged into the ceiling. Didn't take much to get the gun away from her. Once I had her, the rest was easy."

The second elevator dinged and opened. Two security guards came out. While Dad and Steve explained what had happened, one of them shut off the alarm on the elevator.

With his prisoners under guard, Dad turned his attention back to Jennie. "Your mother's resting right now, but I'd like you to wait in her room until I get things taken care of. I think it would be best if we didn't say anything to her about this right now."

"Um . . . Dad, couldn't I just go with you?"

Dad smiled and gave her a what-am-I-going-to-do-with-you look. "You've got your memory back, haven't you?"

"How did you know?"

"Because *you're* back." A light gleamed in his eyes.

Looking at Steve, he said, "I can push the wheelchair if you want to get back to work."

Steve nodded. "Thanks." Turning to Jennie, he added, "And thank you. Your quick thinking saved our lives."

"You're the one who caught them."

Steve left with a promise to provide details for the police report later.

Jennie felt a twinge of panic as she and her father got into the elevator and rode it to the first floor. Fortunately, the security guards had taken the second elevator. They reached the lobby about the same time. When the elevator doors opened, Jennie gasped. Standing there, looking lost and dejected, was the third bank robber. Jennie's heart leaped to her throat as adrenaline once again pumped up her pulse rate. It tamed right down when she realized he wasn't in a position to hurt anyone. Zack was standing in front of Rocky and a uniformed police officer, handcuffed.

The moment he saw Jennie his face slid into a wide grin. "You're okay. I was afraid . . ."

Rocky greeted Jennie and her dad. "I was just coming up to see you two. This guy told me a story you won't believe."

"It's true, Jennie," Zack insisted. "My aunt and uncle were going to kill you and smuggle you out of the hospital on a stretcher. I was supposed to wait in the van for them, but—"

"Shut up, Junior!" Maude let out a string of four-letter words.

He looked surprised when he saw them, then angry. "My name is not Junior. And I'm not going to shut up."

"Let me guess," Rocky said, "these are the crazy aunt and uncle you were telling us about?"

"Yeah."

"I told you he'd crack." Jon's face contorted. "We never should have trusted him."

"Who is he?" Dad directed the question to Rocky.

"His name is Zack," Jennie answered. "He's their

nephew. They forced him into robbing banks, and he was too scared to do anything about it." Jennie glanced up at him. His head was bent, eyes focused on the floor.

"You were right, Jennie. I should have turned them in a long time ago."

"What made you do it now?"

He ducked his head. "I was sitting in the van waiting—praying they wouldn't get to you. I never had much use for God before, but when we were up at the cabin, I started praying for you. Didn't figure there was much else I could do without getting a beating. When we saw on television that you were still alive, I realized God had saved you out there in the woods. Which meant He had to be real. Maude and Jon kept coming up with ways to get to you. They stole a van and delivered flowers to make sure you didn't remember. The flowers were supposed to be bugged, but I took out the listening device when they weren't looking." He sneered at them. "Didn't know that, did you?" His gaze traveled from Dad back to Jennie. "They thought maybe your folks had found it and thrown it away. I started praying for you every day. Every time they tried to kill you, something happened."

"How many times did they try?"

He shrugged. "Four or five."

"When I went to the park with Scott?"

"Right. Maude and Jon took turns watching your house. When she tried to gun you down on the freeway and you escaped that, I knew God had to be answering my prayers. I wanted to call the cops, but I couldn't."

"What made you change your mind?" Jennie asked.

"I was sitting in the van waiting like they'd told me to when these two guys walked by. Rocky said he was going to see you and . . . it was like this voice in my head told me I had to do more than pray. I decided it must be God, so I went after them."

Jennie's gaze met his. "I was praying for you too, Zack. And you're right. God is real."

"That He is." Dad pushed the chair away from the elevator door when some people came. "We'd better get out of here."

––––––––––––

At the police station, Jennie easily identified the trio as the bank robbers who had held her captive and had tried to kill her. Now that her memory was back she'd be able to take the police to the stolen car and explain what had happened during her ordeal. *It's over. They can't hurt you anymore.* Jennie reminded herself of that fact time and again. Still, the experience haunted her with nightmares and flashbacks.

When Scott called two days later, she filled him in on the details he hadn't gleaned from the television news broadcasts. The adults faced long prison terms, and Zack would be doing time in detention and receiving counseling. It wouldn't take much to convince the judge he'd been coerced into a life of crime by his abusive aunt and uncle. Jennie had promised to testify on his behalf. She hoped that intervention would turn him around.

"So what's next for you?" Scott asked. "Got any new crimes to solve?"

Jennie smiled. "I doubt it. My family says after what I've been through, I need a nice long rest."

"Good. Any chance of your coming to the coast?"

"Yep. That's where we're headed this weekend."

"Call me when you get there. I have to work this weekend at the aquarium, but we could hang out together Saturday night."

"Maybe. I'm not sure my parents will let me out of their sight for a while."

"Guess I don't blame them. I'll come up to your Gram's, then."

"Sounds good." They talked a few more minutes, then hung up.

Jennie wasn't sure how she felt about Scott. A lot had changed since she'd lost her memory and regained it. She hadn't believed it possible, but the ordeal she'd gone through and the loss of the baby had pulled her family even closer. The memories of her abduction were vivid and horrifying, overwhelming at times. But Jennie kept reminding herself of the future and all the new, exciting things that lay ahead. Like the party Lisa and her friends were throwing that evening. Jeremiah would be there, and Corisa and Brandy. It would be fun seeing them again.

The future. Jennie didn't bother to suppress the bubble of pure joy that escaped her lips. She walked to her dresser and picked up the card and sweat shirt Gram had given her. The pink sweat shirt had bold purple lettering on it that read, *Of all the things I've lost in this world, I miss my mind the most.* Gram had given it to her the night before, and for the first time since her abduction, Jennie had actually been able to laugh about the memory loss. Gram had presented her with another gift as well. Jennie could hardly wait for Christmas.

"It's time we did something together," Gram had said. *"I've talked it over with your parents, and they agree that you could use an extended break over the holidays. How would you like to go to Ireland with me?"*

Of course, Jennie couldn't say no.

Acknowledgments

A special thanks to Sandy Dengler, Gail Denham, Marion Duckworth, Birdie Etchison, Woodeene Koenig-Bricker, Elsie Larson, Marcia Mitchell, Ruby MacDonald, and Lauraine Snelling for their ongoing help and encouragement.